BACKWATER BLUES

*Thanks to Bob Hudson
and Dave Lambert
for the idea and encouragement;
to Judith Markham
and Lori Walburg
for their seamless editing;
to Charlie Nelson,
Scott Dunbar,
and the late Furry Lewis
for playing the blues;
and to my wife Angelyn,
for everything.*

CHAPTER 1

E-seventh. The prettiest sound in the world. That B note, that D note, and that low rolling E. Yessir.

Old Nick leaned back in the armless wooden chair on his rickety front porch and plucked the throaty, uncluttered E-seventh chord on his guitar. Pure blues.

"Big-legged woman, won't you throw your big leg up on me," he sang, and laughed.

He reached under his chair for the paper sack containing a pint bottle of whiskey, now half empty. "Early Death," his daughter called it. He took a swallow, cleared his throat, set the bottle down, and strummed again. Then he reached in his overalls pocket and pulled out a bottleneck. He played in open E tuning, just right for the bottleneck. He used to use the sawed-off neck of a whiskey bottle, but last Christmas his granddaughter Cindy had given him this stainless steel cylinder from a music store in Hattiesburg. At first he was put off by the slick, shining sound of it, not muted like glass, but he soon came to appreciate its ringing quality and easy slide.

He thumbed the bass E and slid the bottleneck up to the gentlest high B.

"If it wasn't for the woman sold the
    store-bought hair,
That gal I'm loving wouldn't go nowhere,
    Lord knows.
I'm just as blue, blue, blue as I can be.
My gal's got a heart like a rock cast in the sea.
That's the reason why she's so hard to please."

"The St. Louis Blues." He played it like a lullaby. It was a fine spring afternoon in southeast Mississippi. The soft wind blowing through the pines and rippling the clay-red puddles felt sweet on the old man's skin, sweeter still with the taste of whiskey in his mouth and the blues on his tongue and his shoe sole thumping the floor, keeping time.

Nick Rose's shack stood at the dead end of a gravel lane so eroded he could just maneuver his faded turquoise pickup truck down it. He'd lived in this house since the 1940s when he and Effie moved out here to try their hand at cotton farming. They'd managed to buy 140 acres with money he made bootlegging and working on a Mississippi River dredgeboat. The weevils got the cotton after a few years and they couldn't make a living farming, so he'd turned to logging. Except for his half-acre garden, his place had grown up in pine trees, which he cut and sold as he needed to. Now that he was eighty and Effie was gone, he let his sons cut them.

A jaybird flew down the lane screeching. Nick stopped playing and heard the sound of an approaching motor. Moments later a dirty white Oldsmobile pulled into sight, spanning the deep ruts, billowing blue smoke. His great-nephew, Calvin, Joe's boy. Nick sighed unhappily. That boy had trouble in his bones.

Calvin cut the motor and climbed out, tall, handsome, and arrogant in dark glasses and citified clothes. He kicked spitefully at a chicken as he walked up to the porch.

"Hey, old man," he said. "Whatcha got in that sack?" He picked it up and sniffed. "You oughtn't to be drinking this stuff." He turned it up and took a long pull, killing half of what was left. "Man," he whispered, and finished it. Nearly half a pint down the drain, just like that.

"Got any water?"

Nick motioned to the water closet at the end of the porch.

"Why don't you get running water out here?" Calvin said as he dipped well water out of a white enamel bucket. "And electricity. You live like an animal out here, Unk, you know that?" He drank from the dipper and the water ran down both sides of his mouth. "Don't you ever want anything cold, out of a refrigerator?"

"I been satisfied these eighty years. Ain't go'n change now."

"Is that so? Here, let me see this." He snatched the guitar from Nick's reluctant hands and twanged the strings brutally. The old man flinched. Calvin didn't know how to chord it, just struck the open strings.

"I ain't half bad, am I?" Calvin threw his head back and crooned, imitating a blues singer, then

9

handed the instrument back. "Don't you know any rap?"

"What's that?"

"What's that? You don't know what rap is? What century you live in, Unk? Well, anyway, I come over here to see if you got any money I can borrow."

"Ain't got no money."

"I just need a little bit, Unk. Say twenty dollars. All right, ten. I know you got some." He opened the screen door and walked into the house. "Where do you keep it, the sugar jar?"

Nick shook his head as his nephew tramped around the house, fingering his things. The old man picked up his bottle and shook it. Empty. Just a drop. He could remember a day when he'd have cut a man for drinking his whiskey uninvited.

Calvin came back out. "Come on, Unk, where is it?" His voice held a pleading quality. "Here it is the weekend and I ain't got no money. How am I supposed to get any fun?"

"Ever hear of work?"

"Which?"

"Work."

"Aw, come on, old man." Calvin laughed. "I'm gone."

He strutted down the wooden steps, across the bare, chicken-scratched yard, past the big clumps of camellia and jasmine and azalea and wisteria. Effie had set them out when they first moved here.

"Thanks for the whiskey, old man," Calvin yelled as he got in and cranked the car with a grumbling roar, filling the yard with smoke.

The old man went into the house.

CHAPTER 2

Lucinda Sharp headed south out of Hattiesburg, gripping a hamburger in one hand, a soft drink perched precariously beside the gearshift. From the car cassette player 1930s bluesman Robert Johnson sang his wailing, whining blues: "You better come on in my kitchen, 'cause it's going to be rainin' outdoors."

Lucinda—friends called her Cindy—switched lanes in the heavy traffic, simultaneously eating, watching for vehicles, and keeping time with the music. She was twenty years old, angular, graceful, and very dark. Her love for blues had first developed when she was growing up in Philadelphia, Pennsylvania, where she and her mother had moved when Cindy was a toddler. She favored hard-edged country bluesmen like Johnson, Lightnin' Hopkins, and Charlie Patton, but appreciated the softer approaches of Blind Willie McTell and Big Bill Broonzy. Then again, at times nothing would do except low-down city slinkers like Memphis Minnie, Piano Red, and John Lee Hooker.

When she and her mother moved back to Mississippi three years ago after Cindy graduated from high school, she'd been delighted to discover her grandfather Nick was a capable bluesman himself. Strange that her mother had never told her, keeping it to herself like a family secret.

Getting to know her grandfather had been an enjoyable, almost mystically kindred-spirit experience. She liked the old man immediately, though he and his world seemed as foreign to her as someone from another country. It was inconceivable to her that someone in this day and age still lived in a house without electricity or running water—and actually preferred it that way. He wore overalls, clodhoppers, long-sleeved shirts, and a battered, sweat-stained felt hat, even in hot weather. He chewed plug tobacco he bought by the carton and kept a coffee can in his truck for a spittoon, emptying it only when it threatened to slosh over. Once when Cindy had cleaned his truck cab for him, she'd discovered a mouse living under the seat, its sole sustenance a loose plug of tobacco. When she'd shooed it out, it had plopped into the dirt and tried to crawl away, the most pathetic creature she'd ever seen.

From her grandfather's ramblings Cindy learned that he had been a bootlegger in the wild days of his youth. She could tell by a certain look in his eyes that he truly must have been a hard case, but age had softened him. Now he was a man of gentle smiles and kind words.

Twenty-odd miles out of Hattiesburg, she turned off the main highway and headed east into a forbidding and ominous wilderness of pine forests

12

and lonely pastures—a sparsely inhabited, somehow tragic land. Maybe her years in the North had tinged her outlook. From another viewpoint, she acknowledged, the scenery could seem pastoral, even welcoming. Certainly it did not affect her as dramatically as it had when she first moved back to Hattiesburg. She had no real memories of the South, having left so young, yet the smell of pines stirred some aching nostalgia in her.

Mississippi had turned out to be far bigger, somehow, than she had pictured—more lush, beautiful, real. To her the South had always conjured up horror stories of racial violence and backwoods sadism, augmented by movies and books like *Deliverance*, which seemed to revel in portraying rural southerners as some kind of inbred subhumans dwelling in a hellish terrain. These images conflicted with her mother's rare but memorable accounts of her own childhood, descriptions of a wistful wonderland of whippoorwill nights and honeysuckle days. Tugged by extremes, Cindy had trouble finding a middle ground.

Heading down the now well-known route of back roads, she recalled the first time she'd gone to visit Grandpa Nick with her mother. Still in the throes of culture shock, Cindy had been nearly speechless at the foreign surroundings. Already feeling herself to be a different nationality entirely from the native southern blacks she had met—their dialects, their outlook, their very pace were radically different from her own—she had expected her grandfather to be even more bewildering. Yet despite his antiquated ways, he had proved from the start to be warm, humorous, and perceptive. She began to visit on her own after that, bringing him a pint of whiskey in exchange for the blues he played for her. She never came empty-handed.

She turned off into the lane that led directly to her grandfather's place. Her little red sports car handled the rough road with relative ease, since it was small enough to ride the sides rather than having to straddle the ruts down the middle. She pulled up in front of the house and beeped her horn. When she climbed out, she heard her grandfather hollering from behind the house. She walked around back and found him working in the garden.

"Hello, precious," he said as she hugged him and smelled his unwashed old-man smell. "Getting my ground ready to plant."

"Do you plant by the moon?"

He grinned. "Man at the feed store asked me 'bout that moon business. I said I plant when I get the ground ready. I do like to plant by Good Friday, though. It's usually safe, but last year we had some late frost." He shook his head. "Might again this year. It thundered twice last month."

"What does that mean?"

"Thunder in February, frost in April. Don't you know about that, girl?" He adjusted the quid of tobacco in his grizzled cheek. He was never either clean-shaven or fully bearded, as if he shaved once a week. "My Irish potatoes over there are doing pretty good." He motioned with his hoe.

"When do you plant them?" Cindy stepped among the new rows of fresh dirt to the deep-green, glossy potato leaves.

"Valentine's Day."

"What's this over here?"

"Peas. Sugar-snap, they call them. I eat them raw."

"Raw?"

"They're sweet—like candy. Take you a mess of those greens back when you go. Your mama will like them."

"I brought you something, too."

"Too early for drinking, girl."

"Save it for later. Want me to hoe some?"

"Nothing left to hoe. I'm just prettying up these rows. You might go in the house and get a sack so we can pick you a mess of these greens."

"Okay, Grandpa."

After they had picked a sackful, they headed back to the house. Her grandfather moved slowly, almost decisively, and Cindy had to slow her naturally fast pace to stay even with him. He wasn't much taller than she, but even at eighty seemed to contain a coiled power.

"Want a drink of water?" he asked her.

"Sure."

She loved to scoop the tin dipper into the pail of cool well water and sip from it, looking over the ladle through the latticework of the water closet, which was merely a shelf at one end of the porch containing bucket, dipper, basin, and towel.

"The sweetest water never touched pipe," her grandfather said, taking the dipper when she was through and helping himself to a deep drink. "The *sweetest* water never touched metal a-tall. Cedar buckets used to be all we had."

"Cedar sounds good. Here, your bucket's low. I'll fill it up."

"No girl, I'll get that later."

"You sit down, Grandpa. I said I'll get it."

She took the enamel pail to the well, where a tall concrete pipe stuck out of the ground under a small tin roof. The heavy, cracked black-gum windlass was wrapped with old hemp rope. She removed the lid from the curbing and lowered the narrow, shiny, galvanized well bucket. She felt it hit water far down in the earth. A leather valve in the bucket allowed water to flow in from the bottom but not flow out once full.

When the bucket became heavy with water, she cranked it up. The tall cylinder streamed with silvery cool water, which she sloshed into the white enamel porch bucket. Though it was a cool March day, she sweated slightly from the exertion. Pausing, she noticed the low hum of crickets, the breeze in the pine boughs, the erratic tune of a mockingbird.

She hung the galvanized bucket on a nail, covered the well with a saucepan lid, and toted the enamel pail back to the porch, setting it on the shelf and covering it. Then she fetched the pint of whiskey from the car while her grandfather came out of the house with his guitar and settled in his chair at the edge of the porch, in easy spitting distance of the ground.

"Pour me a little in that glass, would you, honey?"

"I thought you said it was too early to drink, Grandpa," she teased, splashing about two fingers of whiskey into a jelly jar and setting it beside him while he tuned up. Then she pulled up an old rocking chair to listen.

The old man took a sip and cleared his throat. He began to nod and tap his foot, stroking the strings at a lazy beat.

"Now the girl I'm loving's
got this great long curly hair,"

he sang in a husky voice.

"Say the woman I'm loving's
got this great long curly hair.
Now her mama and papa
sho don't allow me there."

Cindy recognized the song as a regional variant of "Going to Brownsville." Even as she savored the feel of the blues, a part of her mind analyzed it almost scientifically, codifying it and comparing it with other artists. A major in communications at the University of Southern Mississippi, with tentative aspirations of becoming a television news anchor-woman, Cindy planned to record her grandfather on videotape, hopefully in conjunction with a class project.

In the South she had found few black people her age who appreciated blues. Most of her friends were ignorant of the art form or considered it out of fashion or, worse, a remnant of the Uncle Tom era. It had not been that way in Philadelphia. There her friends, black and white, considered blues timeless and complex, the pure expression of a people, worthy of respect. Bluesmen seemed like prophets, and like prophets they lacked honor in their own country.

"Have you ever heard of Furry Lewis?" Cindy asked when he finished. Lewis had recorded perhaps the most famous version of "Going to Brownsville."

"Where's he from? Wiggins?"

She laughed. "No, Memphis. He's dead now."

Her grandfather shook his head. "I don't know any peoples from Memphis."

"He's a bluesman, Grandpa. Made some records. Was even in a movie or two with Burt Reynolds. You haven't heard of him?"

"No, honey."

"How about Lightnin' Hopkins?"

"Hopkins, Hopkins. There's a Hopkins lives over at Vestry, I believe. Never heard him called Lightnin', though."

"No, Grandpa, Lightnin' Hopkins is from Texas, a famous blues guitarist. He's dead now."

"Why you keep axing me about these dead folks? You think I'm ready to jine 'em?"

She grinned. "No, Grandpa."

"Ain't many bluesmen round here. I met old Scott Dunbar over west of here, near Woodville. And I heard tell of a piano player over round Meadville. Nelson feller. Don't know many bluesmen."

"Did there used to be a lot?"

"Naw, not round here. Most of them's up in the Delta. There was old Kid-Boy Jackson, but they hung him for killing a white man. He played French harp."

"When was that?"

"Back in the thirties. Hung him on the courthouse lawn."

He took another sip and launched into a song.

CHAPTER 3

Calvin arrived at Leon's just as he was getting ready to kill a goat. Calvin had never heard of barbecuing a goat in March, and for some reason the idea irritated him. People barbecued goats in the summertime, preferably the Fourth of July. But Leon claimed he had too many goats and wanted to get rid of one by having this cookout.

On top of that, Calvin discovered, Leon was planning to shoot the goat in the head with a .22 rifle.

"Man, you don't shoot a goat," he said scornfully. "You cut its throat."

The goat was tethered to a rusty swing set behind Leon's house, placidly chewing weeds.

"I don't think the women would like it," Leon said.

Already a group of friends had arrived, bustling around in the house and yard, visiting and drinking beer. A few men clustered around the swing set with Leon and Calvin, while the women were over gabbing with Leon's statuesque wife, Charlene.

"Man, you don't know what women like," Calvin

said, and somebody snickered. "Let's hang this sucker up and bleed him right." He grabbed a piece of rope and lashed it around the goat's hind feet. The animal kicked, but he spoke to it soothingly. Then he untied the neck rope and hoisted the goat hind-first from the crossbar. A couple of the men helped tie it off. The goat swung in the air, bleating with alarm. That caught the women's attention.

"Like this, Leon," Calvin said.

He pulled a big folding knife from his pocket and opened the blade. The thin shine of metal along the edge bespoke its sharpness. He put one hand behind the goat's ears and murmured to it lovingly. With the other hand he laid the blade against the animal's throat, paused a moment, then sliced through flesh and jugular. Blood spattered to the ground.

Leon grabbed a washtub to catch it, and the blood sounded like rain, drumming on the metal. The goat twitched a few times, then became calm and still, its eyes acquiring the glaze of wisdom.

"That's the way you do it, Leon," Calvin said brusquely, looking around for a rag to wipe his knife on. Not a drop had spilled on his hands or clothes. Charlene brought over a paper towel, and he carefully cleaned the blade.

"Now you got to skin and gut it," Calvin said, walking away. "Be careful not to get any hair on the meat." He took a cold beer from an ice chest and mingled with the folks.

By the time the meat was ready it was dark and they were all drunk. Leon had turned on a string of bright electric lights across the backyard. A car radio throbbed deafeningly. The meat was darkly seared and smoky-smelling, dripping with thick sauce. The women set out greens, potato salad, beans, corn on the cob, cornbread, and potato chips. They ate and drank, lounging on the back porch and in lawn chairs.

Unnoticed by the others, Calvin and Charlene slipped around the side of the house where it was completely dark.

When they reappeared sometime later, nonchalantly from opposite sides of the house, they found the rest carrying on a drunken game of volleyball under the lights. Nobody had seemed to notice that the pair had disappeared and returned.

During the game, T-Bone, a short, fat, strong dude, began muscling Leon, who was small and timid and easy to push around. Calvin felt almost affectionate toward Leon now—big brotherly. When T-Bone tripped the smaller man, Calvin shoved the bully. "Watch it, man," he threatened.

T-Bone pulled a foot-long lead pipe from his back pocket and swung it at Calvin's head. Calvin ducked, squirmed sideways, grabbed a net pole, and heaved the mesh over T-Bone's head. He tripped him, shoved him down, and kicked him hard in the ribs and head. That took all the steam out of T-Bone.

Calvin picked up the lead pipe and, with an angry curse, hurled it far out into the darkness. He was perspiring and a button had torn loose from his shirt.

He grabbed one of the last beers from the cooler and left.

Nick's nephew Joe, Calvin's father, reached into his shirt pocket for a toothpick. Inserting it into his mouth, he sat back against a post on Nick's front porch steps, staring idly down the lane.

Nick craned forward and spat a stream of tobacco juice into the yard.

"I got to talk to you, Uncle Nick," Joe said. "About Calvin."

A lifetime of hauling pulpwood had made the short, squat man enormously muscular. He wore dark blue oil-stained trousers, heavy work boots, and a pale blue shirt with sleeves rolled up over his biceps. Nick noticed the gray in the curly hairs at his nephew's temples and felt suddenly tender toward him.

"He been pestering you for money?" Joe continued.

"Why?"

"He's been pestering everybody else is why." Joe sighed and switched the toothpick to the opposite corner of his mouth.

"Calvin's no problem to me," Nick lied.

"There's something wrong with that boy, bad wrong." Joe shook his head.

"Full of mischief," Nick said. "He come by it naturally."

Joe smiled for a moment; then his frown returned. "It's more than that, Uncle Nick. The boy just ain't right in the head."

"What you mean?"

"He likes to hurt things, you know? We ain't never been able to keep cats around the house, 'cause of him."

"You never told me that," Nick said softly.

"I'm worried something's going to happen."

Nick swatted a mosquito.

"Remember his senior year in high school?" Joe's expression softened. "That touchdown pass, homecoming?"

"That boy could sprint."

"And such a good-looking boy! Tall, well-built, like his grandpa. The girls always went for him. His grades weren't no-count, though."

"He did graduate, Joe. Plenty don't."

"You're right. And I believe he could have made good grades if he'd a wanted. He's smart in a cunning sort of way, know what I mean?"

"Like a fox."

"Mink, more like. 'Member that mink got in Pap's henhouse one time? Killed every hen we had, just for the taste of blood. Couldn't eat all them hens." Tears appeared in Joe's eyes. Nick had never seen his nephew cry, except at his father's funeral. The old man spat over the edge of the porch, a bit more gently than usual.

"I keep waiting for the boy to make something of hisself, but it don't look like he ever will," Joe said, rubbing his eyes quickly with his fingertips. "Never could make him do no real work. I thought maybe if he graduated he'd get a regular job, but he won't work that way neither."

"He makes money somehow, though."

"Selling drugs, probably. I ain't blind, Uncle Nick. The boy's trouble-bound." Joe stood up and returned the toothpick to his shirt pocket. "I don't

24

know, maybe if you had a talk with him. You was wild once yourself."

"That's right. I was."

"But you wasn't wild like that," Joe corrected himself. "That ain't wildness. It's something different."

Abruptly, Joe cupped his hands to his mouth and hooted toward the woods, like an owl. A real owl answered, far off.

"Been hearing any turkeys gobble?" Joe asked. "You ought to be able to hear them from your front porch."

"I don't believe I've heard any. I don't pay much attention to them."

"I may get after them this year when the season opens. I haven't fooled with them in years."

"Never did try."

"Well, I'm gone, Uncle Nick. Got saws broke down, truck broke down. Looks like the whole world's falling apart sometimes."

"It do look that way, sometimes," Nick agreed.

Cindy held up her lavender dress and examined it in the mirror. Then she looked at the clock nervously. Ten minutes!

The lavender wouldn't do. She threw it aside, catching a glimpse of herself in blue jeans and T-shirt. Maybe the yellow dress. She snatched it out of the closet and held it up. Too formal.

A knock sounded at the door. He was early! She couldn't meet him like this.

She yanked off her T-shirt and struggled into a floral-print blouse, then hopped into the living room

25

pulling on a pair of tennis shoes. Panting, she smoothed the blouse and opened the door. It was Mrs. Smith, one of her mother's friends.

"Your mama home, darling?"

"She's at the beauty parlor, Mrs. Smith. Due back at five."

The visitor eyed her with a smile. "Getting ready for a date?"

"I'm going to be interviewed, by a reporter for the school newspaper."

"Really! How nice."

"He's due here any minute."

"Well, good luck. Tell Martha I came by."

"Yes ma'am."

Five minutes to four. She wouldn't have time to change. Better to go with what she had on and take the final minutes to tidy up: brush hair, freshen lipstick, hint of cologne. She felt foolish for being so agitated. After all, this wasn't her first interview. But her heart pounded.

Another knock. This time it had to be him.

She opened the door to a handsome young black man. She had not seen him before, only spoken to him on the phone.

"Miss Sharp?" He held out his hand. "Bartram Oliver."

"Glad to meet you." She was cool and composed suddenly, on-stage. Curtains up, lights on. "Come in." She smiled with just the right measure of warmth.

Bartram Oliver, carrying a notepad, followed her into the living room.

"Have a seat," she said. "Care for a Coke? Anything?"

"No, thank you. Really." He sat on the sofa; she perched on a chair across from him.

"You come highly recommended," he said. "Dr. Hofner thinks you hung the moon."

"He's a wonderful teacher."

"How about we start with a biography? Your life story in twenty-five words or less." He grinned. "Or longer, if you like." He held his pencil poised over the pad.

Cindy shifted uncomfortably. She recalled being interviewed as a senior in high school. One passage in the resulting article remained in her mind: "Miss Sharp doesn't just 'talk.' She effuses and enthuses." Cindy had been both flattered and embarrassed by the description, which she had to admit was perfectly accurate. But she was older now, and did not want to come across as quite so—immature.

She peered out the window to collect her thoughts. "I was born here in Hattiesburg," she began slowly. "My family moved to Philadelphia—that's Pennsylvania, not Mississippi—when I was little. I grew up there, and moved back here with my mother after I graduated from high school. I enrolled at the university, and, as you know, I'm majoring in communications."

The scrawl of Bartram Oliver's pencil formed a whisper in the background.

"Communications," he said. "Am I talking to the next Connie Chung?"

She laughed. "Actually, I'm beginning to be more

27

excited by the possibilities of being behind the camera."

"Behind the camera?"

"You know, shooting my own films. Producing."

Oliver nodded. "What kind of films would you like to make?"

"There are so many things! I just can't get over how fascinating the South is. My grandfather, for instance. He's a bluesman, plays the guitar, sings. He's wonderful."

As she spoke, Bartram Oliver's gaze flickered between his pad and her eyes, showing an intense interest in her words. Or was that the way all reporters seemed during an interview?

"He live around here?" he asked.

"South of here, near Wiggins. His name is Nick Rose."

"Hmm. I don't believe I've heard of him."

"He's not famous or anything. He just plays for himself, on his front porch."

"You like the blues?"

"Definitely. We had a blues club up in Philadelphia. We'd all get together and swap albums. Do you like blues?"

He nodded thoughtfully, pausing for a moment in his swift writing. "Yes, especially some of the more modern artists like Freddie King. I also like jazz, some of it. But tell me now, Cindy, what else would you like to film?"

She leaned back, wrapping her hands around one knee as she pondered. "Something on the outdoors. A canoe trip, maybe. Like the one I did on the

Allagash River one time. Great scenery, loads of excitement."

"Like on educational television?"

"Exactly."

"I love ETV." He flipped a page in his notepad. "What are your hobbies—when you have time, I mean?"

"I don't really have any. I like listening to blues, like I said, and I enjoy classical too. I love to read; I read all the time. I used to like to act in school plays, but I haven't done any acting since I've been here. I think theater—I mean real theater—is wonderful. I don't think I have the range for it, or maybe the experience. Anyway—" she realized she was enthusing but plunged ahead, "I enjoy debate. Dr. Hofner really encourages us to open up, be creative."

"What's your favorite book?"

"I just finished *As You Like It* by Shakespeare, and that was really good."

Bartram Oliver shook his head with a grin. "Shakespeare, blues, debate, acting—you're quite a diverse person, Cindy. Do you date anyone?"

She suspected that question wasn't exactly in the line of duty. "My mother gets onto me because I spend so much time at my grandfather's. I go down there every day sometimes, when schoolwork permits. She says I should be out dating, but I don't know. Guys my age seem so shallow, you know? I mean, most of them," she added hastily.

He smiled slightly, closing his notebook. "I'd like to get a picture, if you don't mind. We have the yearbook shot, but I'd like something a little less formal."

"Okay. I just wish I had something else on."

"No, no, that's exactly right. We want to see Cindy Sharp in her natural element. Excuse me while I get my camera."

When he went out to his car, Cindy was surprised to notice her heart beating fast. Maybe it was that question about dating.

"Where should we take it?" Cindy asked when he returned with his camera.

"There's a nice tree out front we could take it by," he said. "I'm really not much of a photographer. Fortunately this camera makes up for my mistakes."

"How about out back? We have a little wrought-iron bench on the patio," Cindy said.

"Great."

She led him through the kitchen and out the back door. "This okay?"

"Fine," he said. "You just sit however you want and I'll shoot."

She perched herself on the edge of the bench, striking a casual but friendly pose. He raised the camera and clicked, moving around to get several different angles.

"Is this a close-up?" she said between her teeth, not breaking her expression. "Maybe I should change shoes."

"No, it's close," he said from behind the camera. "Here, look toward me. That's it."

He finished clicking and lowered the camera, glancing at the film counter. "Those should be great, Cindy."

She smiled and rose. "Can't I get you something to drink? Iced tea?"

"No, really." He took a deep breath. "This sure is some pretty weather we're having."

She sat back down. "Isn't it? My grandfather has all kinds of azaleas and things at his house. I can't wait to see them bloom."

"I love these southern springs," he said. Though the bench was small, he positioned himself on a corner. She scooted over to give him room.

"You're not from here, then?" she asked.

"No. Baltimore."

"Baltimore! Why didn't you say so? I have friends there."

"Really?"

"I didn't think you were from here. You don't talk southern."

He grinned. "You don't either."

"It's a completely different culture down here, don't you think?"

"Man! It's hard to get used to, you know? I mean, I like it—especially the weather. But it's such a different pace."

"And this is a college town. You should see where my grandfather lives."

"What kind of blues does he play?"

"Pure country blues. Do you like country blues? You know, Lightnin' Hopkins, Big Bill Broonzy, Blind Willie McTell."

"I haven't heard a lot of it, to tell the truth. They had a station in Baltimore that played a lot of what I call modern blues, more blues-rock I guess. I used to listen to it a lot. Hey, have you heard that blues

31

show on public radio on Saturday nights? Isn't that great?"

"I stay up for it," Cindy said excitedly. "You know, that emcee, Dr. Bill Ferris, has written a wonderful book on the blues, *Blues from the Delta*. I should have mentioned that in the interview, when you asked me about my favorite book."

Bartram laughed. "Torn between Shakespeare and the 'blues doctor.' You're a trip, Cindy. Do you listen to any jazz?"

"I like some of the early stuff, Dixieland type, mainly 'cause it's a lot like blues."

"Some of this modern stuff, man—" He stopped, hearing someone inside the house.

"That's my mother, home from the beauty parlor," Cindy said.

Bartram stood, reluctantly. "Look, I'd better go."

"No! I mean, there's no need to hurry."

He glanced at his watch. "Hey, it's after five. Boy, time flies."

"When you're having fun." They both laughed.

"Maybe we can talk again sometime," he said. They shook hands, a bit awkwardly.

"Sure. That'd be great," said Cindy. "Come on in and meet my mom before you leave."

———————

Calvin woke up, startled, to find the room filled with light. He heard the eerie wail of a siren, then someone banging on the front door.

"Come on out, Calvin. I've got to talk to you."

He pulled on shirt and pants and went to the door. He kept the screen between himself and the caller,

32

who had left the porch and was standing in the yard. For a moment he thought of trying to escape out the back, then remembered he hadn't broken any laws lately—or had he?—and had no reason to flee. He stepped out into blinding headlights.

"Hey, Calvin." It was Bucky Green, the sheriff's deputy.

"Can't you cut those lights out, man?" Calvin held his arm over his eyes.

"Come on down here and they won't bother you."

He felt his way down the steps, barefoot.

"Calvin, you never paid that speeding ticket from back in January," Green said. "I've got a contempt warrant I've got to serve on you."

"At this time of night?" Calvin thought fast, trying to remember the speeding ticket.

"We run a twenty-four-hour service," Green drawled.

"Hey, the judge said I could wait on that ticket," Calvin said. "I told him I'd have it at the end of this month and he said it'd be all right."

"I don't know nothing about that. I've got this affidavit. That's all I got to go by."

"You can check with him if you want."

"Get your shoes on, Calvin."

When Calvin came back out, Bucky made him lean against the car spread-eagle. He kicked his feet out wide, so he had no balance, and frisked him. Calvin was glad he'd left his knife in the house.

The deputy handcuffed him and put him in the back of the car.

"How long am I go'n be in jail?" Calvin asked as they drove toward town.

"I don't know about that," Bucky said. "Tonight anyway. Until you make some arrangements to pay your fine. You can talk to the judge about it tomorrow."

Calvin was disgusted. A speeding ticket. What justice sent a man to jail for that? At first he'd thought maybe T-Bone had complained about him beating up on him at Leon's. But Bucky hadn't said anything about that. Besides, as he thought about it, T-Bone would never go to the sheriff. Calvin frowned over his miseries, watching the dark wall of pine trees whisk by, broken by starlit pastures.

At the jailhouse the dispatcher, Punky, sat watching television and drinking cola from a quart-sized plastic cup that read "I'm the Boss." Punky and Bucky were being so friendly and nonchalant that Calvin felt unjustly deprived of his right to be angry. But then he'd been through all this rigmarole before.

They emptied his pockets—keys, change, wallet— and took his belt, cataloging each item in a record book and storing them in a locked drawer. Then Punky led him upstairs to the cells. There was only one prisoner in the central lock-up, an old drunk sulled up in a corner. Calvin stretched out on the thin mattress on one of the bunks and tried to sleep.

In the morning they served him a big breakfast, and as he ate he felt almost glad he'd been arrested. They never stinted on food in this jail. A woman cooked breakfast every morning, filling the entire two-story building with the smells of bacon and eggs and coffee.

Later Norwood Oates, the daytime deputy, led him downstairs. Judge Morris, a jolly, oversized, white-haired gent, and Sheriff Marks, who was in his late thirties, were lounging in the dispatcher's office, drinking coffee and swapping jokes.

"Well, well, it's Mr. Calvin," Judge Morris said.

Calvin nodded, cool but not arrogant.

"Why didn't you pay that ticket?" the sheriff asked him.

Calvin grinned. "Forgot about it, Chief."

"Now, Calvin, you know you'll probably get thirty days if you can't come up with the money," said the judge.

"I can't believe my uncle hasn't paid it," Calvin said, making it up as he went along. "You know him—Nick Rose."

"We know Mr. Nick," Sheriff Marks said with a nod, respect in his voice. "But Mr. Nick doesn't owe this fine."

"Naw, naw, he told me he was going to come into town and pay it. Must have forgot. He's getting old, you know."

"I thought you said you forgot it," said the judge.

"Sure, I did. That's 'cause Uncle Nick said he'd take care of it. When he told me that, I just naturally forgot it."

"Well, Calvin," the sheriff said, "if you ask the judge real nice, he might give you till this afternoon to get the money together. That right, Judge?"

"I might."

"Oh, I can get it by this afternoon, sure, no problem. How much is it?"

"It's $165 now, with penalties and all. Sure you can get it by three o'clock?"

"Oh, yes sir, I can get it. No problem. It's just a simple mixup."

The judge and the sheriff grinned at each other. "Three o'clock then, Calvin." The sheriff handed him a tray containing his valuables.

"How am I go'n get back home?"

"I'll run you out there," the sheriff said. "Let's go."

CHAPTER 4

The old man wasn't in his accustomed place on the porch when Calvin drove up, but the pickup was there. As he bounded up the steps, Nick stepped to the screen door, slightly bewildered, like he had been napping.

"Calvin?" he said. He came out, barefoot and bleary-eyed.

The sight of the weak and decrepit old man inspired Calvin with malice, same as the goat had.

"I need money, Unk. No fooling this time."

"Told you, I ain't got no money."

"Come on, where do you keep it?"

Calvin pushed past Nick into the dark, musty house. He hated this house and everything it stood for: the outdated ways, backward thinking, and poverty. Weakness, that's what it was. Old fool of a man clinging to the past. It was always dark in here, lit only by daylight falling through the small windowpanes. It smelled of old lumber and old man.

He went into the kitchen, the brightest room in the house. Old folks always kept their money in the kitchen, among the tins of flour, sugar, and corn meal. He rummaged through the sparsely stocked shelves and cupboards, opening every canister, not bothering to close them. His frustration boiled to near-rage. His indignation at having been arrested slowly turned to focus on his uncle, as though it had been his fault. When the last tin, a can of lard, yielded no cache, he threw it to the floor. It struck the wooden boards and rolled a few feet away, leaving a shiny dent where it had hit.

In the bedroom, a dark, smelly dungeon of rumpled bedclothes and unwashed clothing, he yanked pillows off the bed, overturned the mattress, and opened the old-fashioned wooden wardrobe. He hurled out the few garments: two extra pairs of overalls, a few shirts, and an old dress suit still in its dry-cleaning bag, probably hadn't been worn in twenty years. Opening a cedar chest, he found women's dresses. Did the old fool still keep his wife's things? She'd been dead for years. Or had he been seeing some woman? Calvin dumped the clothing on the floor and shuffled through it. Nothing. Blood pounded at his temples.

He stormed into the living room, where moth-eaten furniture surrounded a coffee table on which sat a dust-covered Bible, a tin-can spittoon, and an empty jelly jar. Calvin looked under seat cushions, then pulled the sofa out, searching for a loose floorboard. Nothing except an old six-ounce Coca-Cola bottle that had rolled behind the sofa who knew how long ago. Calvin picked it up and bounced it lightly in his palm. Then he walked out onto the porch.

Nick was coming out of the woods, pulling up his

overalls. At first Calvin assumed he had gone there to use the outhouse down the path—but then it occurred to him that his uncle must have been hiding his money out there. Smart old fox! That sleepy routine was probably just a trick—and it had worked, almost.

Calvin leaned against a support post on the porch as Nick tottered across the yard and up the steps.

The old man held out his hand. It contained a folded five-dollar bill. Calvin took it, holding it by one corner with disgust.

"Five dollars! This is all you got? Where'd you get it? Is it out in the woods?"

Nick didn't answer. Calvin saw now that it was hopeless. The old man's stubbornness was infinite.

Calvin looked back, spat on the porch, then brought his right hand around and smashed the old man on the temple with the Coke bottle. He grabbed his collar and, opening the screen door with his foot, shoved Nick into the living room, where he collapsed face down on the floor with a grunt. Calvin stood over him, gritting his teeth. He cocked his foot for a kick, then thought better of it. Instead, he walked out and drove away.

CHAPTER 5

Voices rose up in Nick's mind like a devilish wind. It had been one long, eighty-year tumble, and at last with the help of his own blood kin he had reached the bottom. His head raged with pain as if all the simmering fires of a lifetime had erupted in a furious blaze.

From the dark pit to which his life had been reduced, Nick saw the image of his nephew and realized he was seeing himself. The bad news in Calvin's bones was the same force that had powered Nick Rose's life, until he was too old to sustain it. The weapons—knife, razor, gun, lead pipe, baseball bat, or Coke bottle—they were all the same, used on other men. The greed, the hunger, the bloodlust—they were the same, too.

Even when he'd settled down to farming and Effie became a church biddy, he'd stayed mean, nurtured by hard liquor, loose women, card games, parties. Effie had turned to her church meetings and psalm-singing while he stuck with his rowdy ways, staying out all night juking. At first the change in Effie had angered him; when they married she'd been every bit as wild as he. But after a while he got used to it, even when she became ashamed of his music and taught the children to be ashamed too.

Facedown in the abyss Nick saw all the wicked desires burning in his body like a coal fire, producing a slow, steady heat that had consumed everything good. The smoke of his own sins choked him. He burned with the awfulness of the bad deeds he had left on the earth. If this pit opened up now and he tumbled into death, he knew he'd fall straight into the furnace of hell, just as Effie had predicted.

He fancied he could detect her presence above him, an angel weeping over his plight. He imagined her in a white gown holding a hymnal, singing for his redemption. He tried to turn his head to see her but couldn't move. He was paralyzed by pain.

He opened his eyes and realized he must have died, for he saw not the dusty wooden floor but only pure blinding light. He squinted against its glare. He still felt bound and imprisoned, but instead of plunging into fire and darkness he was allowed to stare at this light. It was everywhere, brighter than anything he'd ever seen. He squinted his eyes to try to make out the source of it, and saw something superimposed on it. The thin shadow of a cross lay square across the white light.

A thrill of terror and excitement passed through him. He closed his eyes, unable to endure the purity of the vision with his sick soul, and he wept. He knew now that he wasn't dead just yet. He had been granted a last reprieve, at so late a date, no doubt thanks to the intervention of Effie.

At that instant he knew it was all true, all that

business about Jesus Christ—everything Effie and every preacher he'd ever heard had tried to tell him. "Jesus, Jesus," he said, over and over, a recognition and a prayer. "Forgive me, Jesus." Like a cicada wriggling out of its husk, he felt the years of evil fall away, from the inside out. For however many years he had left, he vowed, he would serve his Savior.

Nick opened his eyes, blinking away the tears that nearly blinded him. He got to his feet slowly. His head throbbed, but the pain was bearable now, a merely physical ache, so much more endurable than the recent agonies of his soul.

He felt strangely happy, looking around him at a new world. The day had been cloudy, but now the sun was out, shining through the windowpanes onto the floor. He stepped unsteadily to the door and peered outside. The glow of sunlight touched the pine trees and bushes and brown chickens and turquoise pickup truck and red gravel driveway curving off through the woods. The sky was blue behind patchy clouds, the air fresh with springtime.

Nick walked to the end of the porch and washed his face in the clean, cool well water.

CHAPTER 6

Calvin was within sight of the main road when, driving too fast, he misjudged and the back end of the car dropped into a rut. He accelerated, but the loose rear wheel spun madly, whipping gravel and burning rubber.

Cursing, he jumped out and kicked the side of the car, venting some of the pent-up rage from his fruitless half-hour search for Nick's hidden money. He tried pushing the car out, but it wouldn't budge. He considered walking back down the lane to Nick's house and taking the old man's truck, but that meant nearly a two-mile walk. What a pain. His fury grew to volcanic proportions, rage mounting on rage, higher than anything he'd ever felt.

Just then, as if in thrall to his earth-shaking anger, an old pickup truck cruising by on the main road stopped and backed up. A white man, farmer by the looks of him, leaned out the window.

"Got trouble?"

With supreme self-control, Calvin managed a sad smile. "I'm stuck."

"Been visiting Mr. Nick, huh?"

"Yessir. He's my great-uncle. I reckon I'll have to walk back to his house and borrow his truck."

The man killed his engine, got out, and walked over. "Wheel dropped off in the rut, huh? I got a chain. We'll just hook her up and yank her out of there."

"Really? Great!"

The farmer backed his truck in, fetched a chain from under the seat, wrapped it around his trailer hitch, then crawled under Calvin's car to attach the other end.

"All right, climb in and crank it," the man said, dusting himself off. "When I give the signal, goose it easy."

"Yessir."

They climbed in their vehicles and started their engines. The farmer eased forward. When he motioned with his hand, Calvin accelerated. The rear wheel caught the edge of the rut and surged forward and out. Once they'd gone a few yards and were on the firm graveled shoulder of the main road, they stopped and the farmer unfastened the chain.

"I sure appreciate it, sure do," Calvin said as the man got back into his truck. "How much I owe you?"

"You don't owe me nothing."

"Here, let me pay you." He offered the five dollars Nick had given him.

"I don't want your money," the man said with pretended testiness. He nodded, put his truck in gear, and drove away.

Calvin watched the truck head down the road, then climbed into his car and followed at a distance.

44

A few miles on, the truck turned into a driveway. Calvin pulled to the side of the road and cut his engine. He heard the farmer slam his truck door and waited to give him time to go inside the house.

Carrying the Coke bottle he'd used on Nick, Calvin walked to the house and knocked gently at the front door. The farmer opened the door, looking at Calvin with mild surprise.

"I just had to give you something," Calvin said.

"Aw, shucks," the man began. "You didn't—"

Calvin swung the bottle and hit him above the eye.

To his shock the farmer, who was short but solid, just stood there. Calvin had the nightmare feeling that the man was impervious to pain. He changed his grip on the bottle and hammered its base straight onto the man's nose. Blood spurted down the man's shirt front and he dropped to his knees, grabbing Calvin for support. Calvin pushed him, and as the man fell back, his fingers tore Calvin's shirt. Furious, Calvin kicked him in the stomach, knocking him backward into the house. Stepping inside, Calvin closed the door and glanced out through the pane to make sure no one was around.

The man lay on his back, his face half-covered with blood, staring at the ceiling. He mumbled plaintively, like a sleepy child. Calvin began screaming curses as rage swept through him in a firestorm. He dropped to one knee and drove the bottle into the man's face repeatedly, until it was a shapeless pulp and his fury had run its course.

Calvin stood up. Staring down at his own bloody clothes and torn shirt, he swore in disgust. He kicked the dead man in the ribs just to pay him back for messing up his clothes. He cursed him again, but his anger had cooled.

Suddenly it occurred to him that someone else might be in the house: an old woman, maybe, or a strong young son hiding in ambush. Gripping the blood-smeared bottle, Calvin crept from room to room, chill-bumps on his skin.

The house was empty.

Intuition told him that the old man lived alone and that he had the whole place to himself for as long as he wanted. It gave him a deep feeling of secret pleasure.

The first thing he did was go into the bathroom, strip, and shower, washing all the blood off. It was on his hands, chest, face, and even in his hair. When he was clean, he rummaged through closets for something that might fit him. In a bedroom that likely belonged to a now-grown son—judging by grinning boyhood photos and old toys—he found some jeans and a T-shirt close to his size. Dressed, he sat on the bed and sighed happily. Then he began going through drawers.

He ransacked the house, checking every possible place for valuables. He finally found some money in a cigar box in a closet, ten one-hundred dollar bills. Fate had dealt him a winning hand, sending that old fool along at just the right moment.

He put the money in his wallet and wadded his blood-stained clothing into a paper sack and walked out into the front hall. The sight of the body startled him; he'd almost forgotten it. A few flies already buzzed around the carnage.

He eased past the body and out the door, stuffed

the sack into the trunk of his car, and headed home. He wanted to shower again, change into his own clothes, and then he'd go pay the sheriff his filthy money. After that he could do anything he wanted. He'd start with a woman, a case of cold beer, and a triple line of cocaine.

CHAPTER 7

"Grandpa? What happened to your head?" Cindy hurried up the steps. Nick sat in his chair on the porch with a book in his lap, a bandage around his head.

"Mule kicked me," he said with a smile.

"A mule! Are you all right?"

He nodded. "I went to the clinic and the lady there bandaged me up."

That part was true. Yesterday when he had realized the seriousness of his injury, he had driven to town, telling the nurse and doctor the same lie about the mule.

"They give me sumpin' 'nother called Tylenol. I done lived all my life without taking even an aspirin. But I guess I'm getting old."

She touched his cheek tenderly. "Are you going to be all right? Did you tell Mother?"

He beamed at the attention but shook his head. "It's nothing, sugar."

"Well, I brought you something." She held up a sack containing a pint of whiskey.

"Don't want it, honey. I done quit all that stuff."

"What? The doctor told you you couldn't drink?"

"The doctor told me sure 'nuff—but not the doctor you think."

She sat down, setting the package on the porch beside her. "Who then?"

"The Grand Physician, honey. Jesus Christ hisself." He pointed to the book he was holding, which she now saw was a Bible. She stared in astonishment.

"I done seen the light. When I got hit in the head, it all become plain, all my evil ways. It was the Lord Jesus giving me one last chance to change my life before it's too late."

"What's wrong with your life that you need to change, Grandpa?"

"Oh, girl, I done some evil things in my time. Your grandpa has been a wicked man." He shook his head. "Your grandma warned me, but I paid her no mind. But Jesus come to me when I was cold on the ground, and I saw what I had to do."

Cindy had read about this kind of spiritual transformation in the lives of many bluesmen, but she couldn't help wondering if in her grandfather's case it had something to do with his head injury. Perhaps he'd been hurt worse than he realized.

"Bring me my guitar, will you, honey?"

She fetched it from the house and sat down beside him again as he tuned up. He began to play and sing at a lively clip:

> "Ah, you just as well to get ready,
>   for you got to die,

For it may be tomorrow, Lord,
    you can't tell the minute or the hour,
Well, you just as well to get ready,
    you got to die.

"So you just well to love your enemy,
    you got to die,
For it may be tomorrow, Lord,
    you can't tell the minute or the hour,
Just as well to get ready,
    you got to die.

"Oh you just well to live a Christian,
    for you got to die,
Then it may be tomorrow, Lord,
    you can't tell the minute or the hour,
Just well to live a Christian,
    you got to die."

He smiled when he finished. "You know, it's a funny thing. I never did play no spirituals, but somehow they're all coming to me, like I been playing them all my life."

"Does that mean you won't play any more blues?"

"I ain't got time for blues no more. Besides, why should I sing the blues? I'm a happy man now."

Rats, Cindy thought. *Now I'm not going to be able to film him.* She had let the chance slip.

Maybe his zeal would fade, though, or maybe she could talk him into a special session of blues later. At any rate, she at least could film him playing spirituals, which in their own way were as traditional and fine as blues. Yet she had never had much taste for spirituals; the ones she'd heard seemed to lack the hard-edged, nitty-gritty quality that made blues so unique.

Nick began to play and sing again. Cindy listened in amazement. As though her grandfather had read her thoughts, he had selected a spiritual with a haunting, minor-keyed, blood-pulsing rhythm.

"Long as I got a seat in the kingdom,
    then that's all right.
You can talk about me as much as you please,
None of your talking going to bend my knees,
Long as I know I got a seat in the kingdom,
    then that's all right."

When he stopped and cleared his throat, she poured him a glass of water from the bucket. He drank. Then he sat quietly, staring out across the yard where the air lay thick and hazy.

"There's a lot of evil in this world, child. Lot of wickedness out there. But I been reading this Bible, and I can see it all spelled out what we're supposed to do. My only regret is it took me so long. All those years Effie kept telling me and I wouldn't listen. I just thank Jesus for giving me this last chance."

Cindy sighed. She admitted to herself that she tended to see her grandfather in ethnological terms, like an anthropologist with a favorite subject, instead of in human terms, one person to another. She probably should be glad he had changed. Yet all along she had felt that the old man was exempt from normal human standards, as though the purity of his music alone absolved him.

"Well, I'm happy for you, Grandpa. You gonna start going to church?"

"I been studying on that. I ain't sure church is where I want to be. I got to do some thinking on that one. I never cared much for church. Bunch of high and mighty people, seems like, looking down their noses at everyone else. That ain't the way Jesus done it. Still—you go to church, don't you?"

"Yessir. I go with Mama."

"Your mama always was a righteous one—a good girl. She followed in her mama's footsteps. I 'spect she'll be glad when she hears about my change."

"She will. She's told me how she prays for you."

Nick reached into his shirt pocket for a plug of tobacco. He pulled the plastic wrapper back, folded down the yellow outer leaf, and tore loose a chunk of dark brown tobacco, inserting it into his mouth.

"Reckon I ought to quit this too. That's what the church people would tell me. That's what your mama would say. But I been doing it too many years. Besides, I ain't seen nothing in the Bible 'bout no chewing tobacco. Jesus didn't say nothing 'bout chewing tobacco. He said love your enemies." His voice trailed off.

"That's the hard part," he resumed. "The drinking and evil living is easy to quit, compared with having to love your enemy."

CHAPTER 8

The pounding on the front door was sharp and vicious. A voice at the open bedroom window shouted, "Calvin, come out of there!"

Ludella sat up in bed. "Calvin!" she screamed, shaking him. Calvin, his head fogged with beer and cocaine, sprang out of bed, confused in the bright morning light. The pounding on the front door did not stop.

"I'm watching you, Calvin," said the voice at the window. It sounded like Norwood Oates, the deputy sheriff. "Don't do nothing. Don't try nothing. Just go open the front door or we'll break it down."

Calvin reached for his pants.

"Leave them!" said the voice.

"Aw, man."

"You can get dressed later."

In his shorts, Calvin went to the front door. Bucky Green barged in, pointing a short-barreled shotgun. "Calvin, you're wanted for the murder of Harvey Blue."

"What you talking about, man? I don't know any Harvey Blue."

"Where were you yesterday after you left the jail?" Bucky asked.

"Uh, I went to Uncle Nick's, just like I said."

"Then where?"

"Then I went to the sheriff's office and paid my fine."

"You a liar," said Green.

"You can ask Uncle Nick," Calvin said, immediately regretting his words.

"We will." Green grabbed his shoulder and hustled him back into the bedroom.

Ludella stood in a corner wrapped in a sheet. "What you doing?" She raised one bare arm threateningly. "We ain't done nothin'."

"Shut up, Ludella!" Calvin said.

In the morning light she didn't look half as good to him as she had last night in the warm glow of cocaine. She made him think of the Pilsbury doughboy—over done.

"Can I get dressed now?" Calvin asked.

Bucky nodded. Norwood, who had been outside the window, came in just as Calvin was pulling on his shirt.

"What about me?" Ludella demanded. "Get out so I can dress!"

"You can get dressed if you want, but we ain't leaving," Green said, his shotgun balanced loosely over his forearm.

"You can at least turn your back, white boy," she said.

"Watch your mouth." But Green turned slightly, watching out of the corner of his eye as Ludella struggled to dress behind the sheet. Norwood searched the room, gathering up Calvin's wallet and car keys.

When the suspects were both dressed, Bucky marched Calvin outside. Norwood followed with Ludella. At the car they frisked Calvin roughly, recited his rights, handcuffed him, and shoved him in back with Ludella. Norwood drove while Green followed in Calvin's car.

At the sheriff's office they questioned him hard. He denied everything. They threatened him with their evidence, mentioning fingerprints, shoe size, tire tracks, and the sizeable wad of bills in his wallet. Then they brought in the bloody clothes and Coke bottle from the trunk of his car. He couldn't believe he'd been so stupid as to leave them in there. It was all Ludella's fault. He'd been sidetracked by her and the cocaine.

When they told him how they'd fetched Nick and heard his story, Calvin knew they had him. Trapped, he finally told them the whole thing, from his trip to Nick's until he left the farmer's house.

In his cell the next morning, Calvin sat and brooded. He was angry—at the cops, at Nick, at Harvey Blue, even at Ludella—at everybody but himself. It was all their fault, not his. He needed money; opportunity came by and he took advantage of it. They should have commended him for not killing old Nick as well. Now they treated him like a criminal. He was caught like a fox in a steel-jawed trap. He'd been in prison once before, six months for aggravated assault. With murder one he was staring at a long stretch, maybe the death penalty.

Punky came upstairs. "Exercise time. Want to go out in the yard?" The yard was a small fenced area behind the jail house where prisoners could play basketball or just sit in the sun.

Calvin had no interest in pacing about like an animal in a cage, but it gave him an idea. "Sure, Punky."

Punky unlocked the door and swung it open. Calvin walked out slow and easy, his eyes darting around, checking everything. He spotted a broom leaning against the wall by his cell where a trusty had left it.

"Trusty didn't sweep too good," Calvin said, staring at the floor. "Look at that." He grabbed the broom as if to clean up the shoddy work, then whipped around and smacked Punky in the head with the handle.

The cheap wood broke in two, and Punky grabbed him. Calvin stabbed blindly with the broken handle, driving the sharp point into Punky's thigh. The man moaned as an arterial flood began soaking his trousers. Calvin elbowed him in the head and raced to the stairs.

He was halfway down when Bucky, hearing Punky's shouts, came running up. Calvin aimed a kick at the deputy's head but caught his shoulder, spinning him around. Then he shoved him, and Green fell headlong down the stairs. Calvin bounded past him and out the side door.

He stood bewildered in the bright sunlight. It had all happened so fast, so unplanned. In another second they would be after him.

He dashed down the sidewalk, rounded a corner

into an alley, and sprinted. He made it to the edge of town before he heard sirens and commotion. He dodged across a field and into the woods, pausing to catch his breath.

As he stared across the field toward the highway, a sheriff's car barreled down the road he had just crossed, and he began to realize his astonishing good fortune. Apparently no one had seen him leave the jail. They had no idea where he was. He was free!

He turned and jogged into the darkness of the woods.

CHAPTER 9

From the porch steps Nick watched the sheriff's car drive away down the lane. Things were happening way too fast. First Calvin had gone crazy and turned against his own kinfolks. Then the sheriff had come out to get Nick and had taken him to the sheriff's office and pestered him with a lot of questions. There Nick had learned that Calvin had killed Harvey Blue. Now the sheriff had just driven up to tell him Calvin had broken jail, leaving a jailer and a deputy hospitalized. Not only that, but the sheriff thought Nick was in danger and had advised him to watch out.

Shaking his head, Nick sank down in his chair. He didn't know what to make of it all. It was almost as if when Calvin had clubbed him down, all of Nick's old evil spirits had left his body and gone straight into Calvin. Because as soon as Calvin left Nick's house, he went and killed Harvey Blue, who as far as Nick knew had never hurt anybody, except for the time he punched Nolan Johns, and Nolan had asked for that.

Nick didn't see why Calvin would come looking for him now, but what with all this evil on the loose, he figured it was entirely possible. There was no telling what Calvin would do now that the wickedness had hold of him.

Nick didn't fear Calvin and he didn't fear death. He had no inclination to go stay with one of his children, as the sheriff had suggested. He was willing to look Calvin in the eye and tell him to get his soul right with the Lord before it was too late, even if Calvin killed him for saying it. But he knew that boy wouldn't listen to his words any more than he had listened to Effie's.

Nick picked up his Bible. Maybe it held the answer. He set the book in his lap and let it fall open at random, sort of like divining for water. He dropped his finger onto the page, then squinted his eyes to read what God had to say to him.

"And immediately the spirit driveth him into the wilderness."

Now that made sense somehow. He'd been wanting to make a fishing trip down Red Creek for some time. He kept promising himself and kept putting it off. He could go and be back in plenty of time to plant his garden on Good Friday. There was nothing he had to do between now and then.

He knew a place on Red Creek way back in the woods with some good fishing holes. He'd load his truck with fishing equipment and camp out. The Spirit would tell him when it was time to quit fishing and go home.

"Thank you, Lord," he mumbled.

CHAPTER 10

Beethoven's *Pastoral* Symphony filled the car as Cindy sped south. The sweet energy of the classical music was just what she needed today, which she loved second only to blues. It formed a needed contrast, yin and yang for her musical soul.

Spring break was here at last, and she was determined to film her grandfather playing his music. She had a videocamera in the back seat, ready to begin today, hopefully followed by several more sessions this week. With a little luck she might coax a blues segment out of him just for old times' sake.

Nick was out fussing around his pickup truck when she drove up.

"Whatcha doing, Gramps?" She kissed his grizzled cheek.

"Getting ready to go fishing," he replied, arching his back in a stretch and surveying the pure blue sky. "This warm weather ought to have the fish stirring."

"I brought you a present," she said, handing him a package. "This is something I know you'll like."

"What is it?" He pulled out a huge book.

"It's a large-print Bible, Grandpa. It'll make it easier for you to read."

He opened it and took a look. "Why, it will, sure 'nuff. Thank you, honey. You sure didn't have to do this."

"I know I didn't have to, but I wanted to."

He set the Bible in the cab of the truck. "I'll take it with me."

She looked in the back of his truck at the array of lines, hooks, lead weights, and other accessories, all heaped in a cardboard box. "I thought people went fishing early in the morning."

"Catfish feed at night, sugar. Besides, I plan to be gone a spell."

"Really? How long?"

He shrugged. "Till I feel like coming back. A few days, anyway."

"Oh, Grandpa," she said, crestfallen. "I'd hoped to film you this week. I'm out of school all week on spring break and I thought I could finally get around to putting your music on film."

He shook his head with determination. "Fish are biting. You got to go when fish are biting." He walked toward the house.

"Where do you fish?" she asked, following.

"Out on Red Creek."

"You're going to camp out?"

"That's right."

"I used to do a lot of camping up north. Canoeing too. Some friends and I went canoeing once on the Allagash River in northern Maine."

They went in. She trailed behind as he rounded up his camping equipment.

"I wish I could go," Cindy said. "I love to camp."

"Well, I 'spect it'd be kind of rough on a girl like you."

She laughed. "I know what it's like to rough it, Grandpa. I hiked four days once on the Appalachian Trail. That's in the mountains, you know. And we spent a week on the Allagash. I didn't catch any fish, I admit. I'm no fisherman. But I loved the camping out."

He turned to her with a slight grin. "Didn't catch no fish, huh?"

"No sir."

"It must run in the family." He shook his head as they toted gear out to the truck. "I never was no count at catching fish. I got the know-how; I just don't have the touch."

He grunted as he heaved a loaded duffel bag into the back of the truck, then paused to stuff a chew of tobacco into his mouth. "Seems like in this life know-how ain't enough. You got to have the touch. Touch and know-how."

"You sure have the touch when it comes to playing guitar."

"I reckon. Little bit anyhow." He rummaged through his truckload of equipment. "I'm still short a few things. Got to go see if I can find a boat paddle in the barn."

"Paddle? You have a boat?"

"I used to anyways. Kept it down by the creek. I haven't checked it in over a year. I hope it's still there. I got the plug so I don't reckon anybody stole it."

"What kind of boat is it?"

"Flatbottom."

"Is that like a pirogue?"

"Bateau, some people call it. A pirogue's different. Littler, narrow, pointy ends."

"How big is your boat?"

"Not but ten foot."

"Is that big enough?"

They went around to the barn. "What you talking about? That's plenty big."

The barn smelled of hay and old lumber. "I used to have an ice chest back here too," Nick said, pulling a pair of weathered boat paddles from a stack of rough cypress boards. He walked into a dark stall past hanging harnesses and mule collars, their leather cracked and mildewed. Then he came out shaking his head. "Can't find it."

"I have an ice chest, Grandpa. What do you need it for, soft drinks?"

He laughed. "Need it for fish, honey, if I catch any."

"Grandpa, why don't you let me go with you? I've got all the equipment I'll need, and I can get an ice chest. Mama's got one. I've camped all over the Northeast but never camped in the South and I've always wanted to."

He studied her with an amused expression. "Baby, I don't know. You sure you're your mama's child?"

She laughed.

"'Cause your mama wouldn't have gone camping for anything in this world. I took her once when she was a chap." He shook his head. "She cried most of the time. Scared the fish away."

"I promise I like camping. I've been plenty of

times. And I have the whole week off. I can run home and round up my stuff and get whatever you need and meet you back here."

"I don't know. It seems sort of a durnfool thing to do, taking a little girl like you." She saw he was teasing. "But I guess if you cry too much I can just bring you back to the house."

She hugged him. "Thanks, Grandpa. I'll go get my stuff. Tell me what you need."

He pondered. "A loaf of light bread. Some ice for the ice chest. If you're going by a bait store it wouldn't hurt to pick up some big fat night crawlers."

"What's that?"

"Worms, honey. And if you're going to be stopping at a store anyway, you might get me a carton of Cannonball tobacco." He fished in his pocket and drew out a rumpled twenty-dollar bill.

"I'll take care of it, Grandpa," she said, refusing it.

But he insisted, so she took the money and headed back to Hattiesburg. The filming would have to wait.

CHAPTER 11

Calvin and Ludella sat by the little muddy creek that flowed through the woods behind her house. "What I need is a plan," Calvin said.

Ludella sucked on a marijuana cigarette and handed it to him. "What about that uncle of yours?" she asked in a voice ludicrously strained from holding her breath. She exhaled forcibly, a stream of pungent smoke that disappeared in a sudden gust.

Calvin nodded. "That's what I'm thinking. I can't go home. They got my car, my money, everything. I know that old man's got a stash, plenty of it. Look at him, sitting pretty on all that land he owns. Never spends a dime except for chewing tobacco and whiskey. No electric bills, no water bills, grows nearly everything he eats. He's got to be loaded with jack."

He sipped the smoke and stared at a yellow and black butterfly wobbling over the creek. "I get over there, I can load my pockets with money, take that old truck of his, and leave this lousy place."

"What if the sheriff's watching?" She took the cigarette from him.

"Why should he watch an old man like that? Besides, I'll be careful. Go in at night. I need you to take me, Ludella. You can just drop me off at the driveway and I'll walk the rest of the way in." He lay back, resting his head in his hands, staring at the milky blue sky through the bare branches. A few were putting out green buds.

"You ain't go'n do nothing to him, are you?"

"Naw." He retrieved the joint and smoked it to the coal, then tossed it into the creek, where it sputtered and floated. "Got another joint?"

"That's it."

He was high but not enough. He was never high enough—except when he'd done the job on that white man. The memory made him tingle. He turned to Ludella, who sat with her knees drawn up staring at the creek. "You know what it's like to do a guy?"

"Kind of like being high?" Her mouth stretched in a grin, her eyes glazed.

He looked again at the sky. Foolish women. Couldn't expect them to understand. Killing was man's business.

"You's scary sometimes; you know that, honey?" she said, staring at him.

He laughed, and his laughter seemed to emerge as bubbles from his mouth. The marijuana was stronger than he'd thought. "Fear is nothing but the beginning of happiness," he told her.

"They go'n be looking for you soon, babe."

"Sure they will. But they won't catch me. They can't hold me. Ain't nobody can hold me, Ludella. After I get clear, I can come get you." He was lying, but so what? "We can head down to the coast, you and me. Biloxi. Or better yet, Florida. Once I get that old man's stash, sugar, we're home free. Let's get out of Mississippi."

"Out of Mississippi?"

He put his hand on her leg, turning on his side to face her.

"Calvin, wait a minute. You scaring me."

He pushed her down and moved in close. "I told you, fear is the way to happiness. Don't you listen, Ludella?" There was a hard edge in his voice. He kneaded her leg with strong fingers.

Insects moaned around them, the thin-voiced crickets of March, and Ludella felt she was at the center of a whirlpool, surrounded by slowly spinning sky and branches, the creek murmuring an angry staccato in the background. Calvin crushed her mouth in a kiss. She felt like a fly grabbed by a spider.

Ludella did not resist; she was already paralyzed, the marijuana fogging her brain. Lying on her back on the cold, damp ground, she stared up past his dark shape into the mesh of tree limbs encasing her hopelessly.

CHAPTER 12

"Cindy, telephone!" her mother called.

"I'm trying to get ready. Oh, okay." Cindy hurried to the phone. "Hello?"

"Cindy? This is Bartram Oliver." His warm, languorous tone contrasted with her rushed pace.

"Hey, Bartram," she said, taking a breath to slow herself down. "What's going on?"

"I just called to tell you about the article. They want to run it in April, a special section on interesting students. I had hoped to get it in sooner."

"That's fine. How did the pictures turn out?"

"Great! Despite the photographer. The camera and your looks made up for my lack of skill. You're very photogenic."

She smiled. "I'll bet you're an excellent photographer."

"Look, I wanted to ask you—I know this is short notice—but are you free tonight? A classical guitarist is playing on campus and there are still plenty of seats."

"Oh, Bartram, I wish I could," she said, "but I promised my grandfather I would go fishing with him. I'm just getting my stuff together right now, in fact."

"Fishing? I don't picture you as the type."

"What was that you called me? Diverse?"

He laughed. "I had that right. Well, maybe we can go out another time."

"I'd like that. Just call me. I'll be gone a day or two, maybe three."

"Three days?"

"We're camping out."

She heard him chuckle. "Okay, I'll check with you later then," he said. "If you want to see these pictures before the story runs, I'd be glad to bring them by."

"Oh, no, that's all right," she said, then reconsidered. "Still, if you wouldn't mind bringing them by. Look, how about I just call you when I get back; then we can set something up?"

"Great," he said and gave her his home phone number. "I'll look forward to hearing from you. Have fun, now. Catch a lot of fish."

"Okay, thanks. Good-bye."

After she hung up, she caught herself gazing at the phone with a smile. Then she remembered the camping trip and hurried to finish packing.

———

Cindy gripped the side of the truck as it bounced down the poorest excuse for a road she'd ever seen—if two ruts in a corridor of high grass could even be called a road. They passed into dark river-bottom woods where standing water gleamed dully among huge oak, beech, and cypress trees. Nick guided the truck gingerly through a mudhole she would never have dared, the tires shimmying through the sloshing gumbo. Then the forest opened to reveal a wide, white sandbar along the creek.

Nick cut the engine. "This is it."

Cindy jumped out, ready for anything. She was dressed in her thickest blue jeans, a long-sleeved pale blue cotton work shirt—prison shirt, her mother called it—and her old white sneakers.

Her grandfather, wearing black rubber boots along with his usual overalls and felt hat, rummaged in the bushes. "Here it is!"

She saw a battered, upturned aluminum boat tied to a tree with a thick rope. He untied it, and she helped him carry it down to the sandbar near the water's edge. He screwed in the boat plug, and they brought down the paddles and fishing gear from the truck.

"We'll camp here by the truck," Nick said.

"I've got a tent."

"You use whatever you're used to. I got an old tarpaulin I use."

Cindy pitched her yellow and brown tent in the white sand, while her grandfather strung his tarpaulin into a lean-to beside the truck.

When they finished, she strolled down to inspect the creek. "This is beautiful, Grandpa," she said as he joined her. "I'm glad I brought my swimsuit."

He chuckled. "River's too cold for swimming this time of year, girl. It's March yet."

She knelt down and put her hand in the clear water, which ran over sand and pebbles. "It's cold, but not as cold as the Allagash."

"Suit yourself."

"What do we do now?" she asked, eyeing the sun standing just over the treetops.

"We got an hour or so before we need to get the lines out," he said. "Bait them too early and bream'll eat the bait off. Got to bait them just at dark. Catfish start feeding at night. We'll check them tonight and in the morning."

"Do we fish here?"

"Got to fish the deep holes. Down the creek a little ways, right around that bend, is a powerful deep hole. Used to be an old bridge. Nothing left but pilings now. That's the best spot. We'll put out a trotline there. And there's some other holes hereabouts too."

"Trotline? Is that what you catch trout on?"

He laughed. "Catfish. You'll learn about it soon enough."

He began to organize his fishing equipment while she stepped behind the truck and changed into her swimsuit. The day was warm enough, but the breeze held a chill. She scampered across the sandbar and waded in.

"It's cold!"

"I told you," said the old man, kneeling beside the boat sharpening hooks. "This creek is spring-fed mostly. It's cold in August even."

She plunged out and swam to deep water. Treading, she sniffed the sweet river smell and gazed at the tall trees along the high bluff across the creek. She ducked under and came up breathless from the cold. Her laughter echoed across the water. She felt fully alive.

Calvin cursed when he realized the old man wasn't home. He was panting, having jogged down the lane after Ludella let him off at the road. Nick's house was dark, the door locked with a cheap padlock, though it was easy enough to get inside since the old fool left his windows open. All he had to do was remove a screen.

The presence of the strange red sports car in the driveway had alarmed him at first, making him wonder if there was an ambush. But the place was unmistakably empty. Where was the old geezer? Probably gone off drinking with one of his cronies. That meant he'd be back late.

Calvin lit a candle and went into the kitchen to rummage for something to eat. Almost no food, and no refrigerator. Not even a decent stove to cook on— just an old woodstove. He found some dry biscuits and salt meat to snack on, washing them down with well water, then sat in the dark living room to wait.

He should have made Ludella drive him to the house and stay with him. He could have sent her out for beer and chicken. No, on second thought, he was sick of Ludella. He didn't like to be with any one woman too long. But he could sure use her wheels. Now he was stuck in this shack with nowhere to go, no way to get there, and nothing decent to eat.

He fell asleep on the sofa and woke late in the morning, fiercely hungry. Searching through the old man's cupboards again, he discovered a quart of home-canned tomatoes and ate it all, drinking the juice. He also spotted a shotgun propped in the back corner of the kitchen, a box of shells beside it. He stuffed the shells into his pocket and carried the gun outside with him, stopping to wash his face with water from the bucket on the porch.

As he turned to walk down the steps, he noticed a paper sack beside the old man's chair. In it he discovered an unopened pint of whiskey.

"My luck ain't run out yet," he muttered, breaking the seal. He took a short swig to rinse his mouth and stuck the bottle in his back pocket. Then he went down the steps to check out the car.

It was locked tight, one of those new ones that were hard to break into without the proper tools. Kicking gravel across the driveway in disgust, he spotted something metallic on the ground. It was a fishhook.

Something clicked in his mind.

Fishhook. Right. The old man always went fishing in the spring. Now where would he have gone? Calvin remembered his father talking about going fishing with Nick on Red Creek. There weren't many places where you could get to the creek. He'd just have to do some exploring.

Gloating, he stretched and set about the serious task of breaking into and hot-wiring the car. His luck hadn't run out yet.

CHAPTER 13

The old man's headlamp filled the night with crawling shapes. The johnboat drifted down to a bend, and the two paddled hard to swing with the current and miss a snaky-looking pool under a high bank.

"We may come back by that hole," Nick said. "I've caught a few fish there before."

The river chimed with the sounds of running water and piping rainfrogs, pulsing with the deeper croaks of bullfrogs. The air smelled of sweet water, woodland mist, and the mosquito repellent Cindy had sprayed on. She saw the river in shades of black and white as the light bobbed with every turn of her grandfather's head, throwing grotesque shadows around them, illuminating overturned trees like recumbent monsters with their arms in the air, pairs of green eyes the size of pinpricks and red eyes like marbles, fallen logs slick as the backs of river pythons. Cindy shivered; she loved it.

They rounded another bend. "Up here," Nick said. She turned to look at him but the light blinded her. "Paddle over under that bluff."

74

They stopped at the base of a high clay bank, the stern swinging around to rest against a log. "I'm going to tie one to this here log," Nick said, his headlight pooling around his rubber boots as he bent over to gather his fishing gear. "We'll paddle across to that limb over there and tie it off."

Cindy waited patiently until he nudged the boat forward, then she joined him in paddling. The boat moved across the smooth, mist-covered water.

"This hole is some deep, child. Used to be a bridge here, but you can't tell it now."

They stopped at a limb rising from a submerged log, bobbing gently in the current, and Nick tied the other end of the trotline to it.

"Now I need you to grab hold of that line and ease us across a little at a time. Whoa. There."

Cindy held the cold, wet cord while Nick attached a hook to each looped string that dangled from the main line. He tied a couple of heavy weights onto the line as well.

"Now we got to go back and bait them," he said.

They repeated the process, slower this time as he slid fat, wriggling worms onto the hooks. When they came to the end, he dropped the line. The dark water swallowed it up.

"This is a good hole, sugar. We're go'n catch some fish tonight. Feel how still it is?" He held out his palm. "Fish'll be feeding tonight."

They drifted downstream to the next hole, and Nick put out another trotline, then paddled back upstream, where he put out a third and a fourth. The going was easy except when they entered bends where the current was stiff. As they paddled up the last stretch toward their camp, the river began to hiss with raindrops. Cindy reached for her poncho and pulled it on, tugging the hood up as the rain increased. The shower ended before they got back to camp.

They dragged the boat up on the sandbar. Nick stirred the embers of their campfire and added some limbs until it flared to life.

"It's chilly out here," Cindy said, standing close to the blaze.

"It's this March air. We're lucky it's so still. It'll get windy before the month is out."

Cindy poked at the fire with her soaking, dirty tennis shoes.

"You glad you came?" Nick asked. "Or do you wish you were home in a dry bed about now?"

She grinned. "I love it out here, Grandpa." She looked up at the few stars visible through the river mist. "I've never been anywhere like it."

"This is a fine creek." He sat on the ice chest, the collar of his denim coat turned up, his rugged features shadowed in the firelight. "Runs into the Pascagoula River. Well, that ain't right, exactly. First it runs into Black Creek. Then they both run into the Pascagoula. Now that's a fishing river. They got catfish in there as big as you are."

She looked at him incredulously.

"Yessir, they do," he insisted. "Ain't many caught; line won't hold 'em. But ever so often somebody'll bring one in."

"What's the biggest fish you ever caught?"

"I caught a bluecat in the Mississippi River once that weighed forty-two pounds. I've seen them go as high as seventy, seventy-five pounds. Spotted cat. Great big things. Now on this creek I never caught nothing more than, oh, twenty-five pounds. The big ones in here swim up from the Pascagoula. It's a big swamp down there, child. I never fished it. I'd like to someday."

"Aw, we should have brought your guitar," she said suddenly.

"Night air ain't good for it. I'll play when we get back. You might get some sleep right now, girl. We got to check them lines in two-three hours."

"I'm not sleepy, Grandpa."

"I think I'll go catch a couple winks."

He went to his lean-to while Cindy sat by the fire, watching castles in the embers.

They ran the lines twice that night, catching several catfish, a soft-shelled turtle, and a bass. At first light Cindy made coffee while Nick slung a cord over a tree limb and ran it through a catfish's lower jaw.

"Here, Grandpa," Cindy said, handing him an enamel cup full of strong, hot brew.

"Well now," he said, pausing to blow the steam and sip gingerly. He smacked his lips. "Mighty fine." Then he set the cup on a log and resumed his work. "You brought me good luck, girl. This one here'll weigh fifteen pounds."

"Really? Wow!" She studied his movements. "I've never seen anybody clean a fish like that."

"Just you watch." He showed her how to make slits in the skin and how to wield the catfish pliers.

When he had peeled the hide off and cut the filets out, he strung up another fish, handing her the tools. "Now you do it."

She went to work while he drank his coffee and watched. Rain began to sprinkle but she ignored it, concentrating on her task. The legs of her jeans were soaked and smeared with mud and sand, her hands were slimy and smelly from fish, and the sleeves of her prison shirt dangled loose. She felt rumpled and sleepy.

Nick helped her cut the filets out, then handed her the strips of translucent pink flesh. "Here. Batter these with corn meal and salt and fry them up in a skillet of hot grease while I finish. Those coals should be just about right."

Cindy poured herself another cup of coffee from the big enamel pot and started breakfast. Nick finished his cleaning just in time to wash up at the creek and sit down to a huge plate of fresh-fried catfish with white bread and more hot coffee.

"What do we do today?" Cindy said when she finished, sitting back.

"Do a little bream fishing, I reckon. We'll cut ourselves a couple of cane poles and round up a few crickets. Plus I need to put the minnow bucket out to catch shiners for tonight. Wish we had some more of them night crawlers. Where'd you get them?"

She named a bait shop south of Hattiesburg. When she told him what they cost he whistled.

"What'll you do with the fish, Grandpa? The ice chest will hardly hold them all."

"First thing we got to do is eat." He patted his belly. "Eat and then eat some more. When we got more than we can handle, I'll carry a load out to Mr. Johnson's store on the highway. He'll take them off my hands. He's always on the lookout for fresh fish."

That day they did some creekbank bream fishing, which gave Cindy an excuse for an extended nap. At noon they cooked the turtle with gravy and ate it over bread. In the afternoon Nick showed her how to bait the minnow trap with clumps of bread and how to use the dip net to catch crawfish in the puddles back in the woods for more live bait. Then they slept, ate a big supper of fried bass and more turtle, and set out at dark to bait the hooks before running the lines that night.

By now Cindy felt pleasantly fatigued, her body loose and supple, her head clear, her lungs fresh with river air. Happy to be with her grandfather and to be fishing, she felt prepared to stay out here all week.

She felt a tang of regret at the thought of the missed concert with Oliver. No matter; she would see him when she got back. That thought just made her happier.

In the morning when she woke she was surprised to see how late it was. She had expected her grandfather to wake her at dawn as he had the day before.

"Grandpa?" she called as she climbed out of her tent.

He was sitting on the ice chest, his new Bible open in his lap, frowning as he ran his finger across the text.

"Why didn't you get me up? Are you all right?"

He glanced up, preoccupied, then shook his head. "I had a bad dream. An evil dream. I had to think it out."

She knelt by the coffeepot and poured herself a cup. "What about the fish? Didn't you need me to help you skin them?"

"I skint them, honey. I just needed to study on this here dream."

"What was your dream, Grandpa?" she asked softly.

"I dreamt a plague of locusts swarmed up out of Wiggins in a black cloud and was coming down the river toward us. I was standing right there on the sandbar looking at it. At first I wasn't worried none, 'cause what do I care about locusts? But then the cloud began to take the shape of a person, and I realized it was coming to get *me*." He shook his head.

"It sounds like you ate too much fried fish before bed." Cindy laughed, but the old man remained solemn.

"So I got my Bible out." He tapped the big book she had given him. "This here's got the answer to any problem if you know how to use it. I fixed a pot of coffee and sat down here and said a little prayer and then I just let the Bible fall open where it would."

"And? Where did it fall open?"

He flipped through the pages. "Right here. Listen: 'The third angel sounded his trumpet, and a great star, blazing like a torch, fell from the sky on a third of the rivers and on the springs of water.' Revelations 8:10."

Cindy frowned. "So what does that mean?"

"Well, that's what I asked myself. I studied on it. The angel that sounded—I reckon that's the dream God give me in my sleep. Now the star that fell from the sky, everybody knows that's Lucifer, the devil. In other words, that's evil, some evil spirit or evil person—just like I dreamed, don't you see?"

"What about the rivers?"

"I wasn't so clear about that. But so far I knew I was on the right track, because the Scripture just backed up my dream. So I let the Bible fall open again." He turned the pages. "This here's what I read: 'I'm going out to fish,' Simon Peter told them." He closed the book with an air of finality.

"I'm afraid I don't understand," Cindy said.

"I didn't neither, at first. I thought, I'm already fishing. Why should it tell me to go fishing when I already am? Then I remembered the part about the third of the rivers. That's when I understood. The third of the rivers, you see, that's the Pascagoula—the lower Pascagoula, I suspect. You see, Red Creek is the first of the rivers. Where it joins Black Creek is the second. And the Pascagoula is the third. You see?"

"Not really."

"The Scripture is telling me to go fishing on the third of the rivers—that's the Pascagoula. We got to pack up and head downriver."

She shook her head and laughed uncomfortably. "Grandpa, I really don't think that's how we're supposed to read the Scripture, you know? I just don't think—"

He wasn't listening. "I thought about driving down there, but the plainest thing is just to take in our lines and float down. Of course, if you don't want to go, honey, I'll take you back to your car. Or you can take my truck."

"But if you float down to the Pascagoula, how will you get back? You can't paddle all that way upstream, can you?"

"I don't have to open the Bible to know the answer to that. 'The Lord will provide.'"

Cindy felt frightened. She had placed such faith in her grandfather's levelheadedness. Now he sounded senile. The man who a week ago was playing down-home blues and sipping whiskey was now drawing all sorts of strange messages from the Bible. What on earth had happened?

The only explanation she could think of was the blow to the head he had sustained when the mule kicked him. It must have affected his mind—which was understandable, particularly at his age.

"I really don't think we should do it. Not now anyway, Grandpa," Cindy said. "Maybe if we planned it out somehow and had someone to pick us up when we got down there—"

He stood up, a slight smile on his face, as if he possessed secret knowledge. "You take my truck and go on back, honey. Your old grandpa will be all right."

"No," she said, suddenly perceiving the extent of his vulnerability. She went to him and put her arms around him. "I'll go with you, Grandpa."

He patted her back, and when she looked at him she saw tears running down his face, even though he was smiling. "Maybe you're the angel," he said.

She laughed, surprised to find tears in her own eyes.

CHAPTER 14

After Red Creek merged with Black, the stream became wide and slow. They passed small house-boats used for fishing camps, but since it was neither weekend nor holiday every camp was deserted. It gave Cindy an eerie feeling to glide past the vacant dwellings in this wilderness of swamp and forest.

The peacefulness she had felt at their upriver camp was gone. It had vanished the instant she recognized her grandfather's unsoundness of mind—and when she'd realized it was up to her to look after him. He would not be persuaded to abandon his plans, though she'd tried subtly as they packed up camp. Before they set out downriver, she'd made one last straightforward plea. He just smiled and shook his head with that blissful look of divine inspiration and once again offered to let her take his truck home.

And suppose she'd done that? Occasionally she read in the papers about elderly people wandering off and being found days later, sometimes dead of exposure. The turn he had taken probably wasn't so uncommon among the elderly. Whatever chemical forces worked on the aging brain had obviously eroded his mind, no doubt triggered by the blow to his head. If she'd left him, he would have drifted downriver until—well, she didn't want to think about it.

She had even entertained the notion of letting him go while she fetched help. But she feared that once he set off down that creek, they might never find him. The easiest course was just to go with him. As for how to get him back, she'd cross that bridge when she got to it. Maybe at some downstream town she could phone her mother and have her come pick them up. She doubted they could paddle all the way back.

The best thing to do for now was enjoy the trip through these southern swamps. That shouldn't be too hard. The sky was perfectly blue with a purity that made her think of the Mediterranean and the Arctic, though she had been to neither place. The trees—fewer pine now, more cypress and syca-more—were putting out tiny new buds. They appeared to be draped in silvery green gauze. Except for sleepy-sounding crickets, whose tones flowed in waves, the creek and woods were silent.

As they paddled, easily and in rhythm, her grandfather began to sing spirituals. His low, rich voice soothed away her cares. Gradually her awareness diminished—or expanded—until it encompassed only the present moment, this place of woods and water, the feel of the air on her skin, the sound of the old man's voice behind her backed by a choir of insects. She closed her eyes to savor the sunshine on her face.

They stopped to eat lunch on the porch of one of the floating camps tethered to a tree, for the woods were too soggy to go ashore. Their pace was slow in the sluggish current, and it was late in the day when they reached the Pascagoula River, a wide, muddy stream with the sweet stink of swamp.

Late afternoon sunlight sloped over the high wooded bluffs to their right, and Cindy began to worry again when she failed to spot a suitable campsite. On one side were fifty-foot bluffs; on the other, swamp. No sandbars, no dry, open woods.

Suddenly she caught the sound of distant traffic and wondered if she could now talk her grandfather into going home. She could phone her mother, and they wouldn't have to deal with the problem of camping in this swamp. She heard the rhythmic clatter of vehicles passing over a bridge, and began planning her strategy. She would suggest they stop to rest at the bridge, and when they were ashore she would use all her powers of persuasion. Maybe her grandfather would be tired enough by then to quit; maybe the power of his divine revelations would have faded.

Still, she felt challenged by this wilderness of southern wetland. If the circumstances were different—if she had a younger, stronger companion—she would like to explore it, especially in a canoe. Later, maybe.

They rounded a wide bend and she spotted the tall concrete legs of a bridge up ahead.

"How are you doing?" she said, turning to look at her grandfather.

He smiled, showing the stain of tobacco juice on his yellowed teeth. He wore his denim jacket despite the warm sunshine. "Good, honey."

She stretched. "I'm getting kind of stiff. Can we stop up here under this bridge?"

"Sure thing, baby."

As they approached the left side of the bridge, Cindy noticed a man sitting at the water's edge with a fishing pole. When they drew closer, she saw it was not a fishing pole but a gun. Was hunting season open?

"Lord, Lord," her grandfather mumbled in alarm. "The Lord done delivered me into his hands."

Cindy looked at her grandfather questioningly, then at the young black man, now standing, on the bank under the bridge. "What's the matter, Grandpa? Who is it?"

The current, swift under the pilings, swept them in close, and the stranger stretched out precariously to grab the boat.

"Howdy, Unk. What took you so long?"

"Who are you?" Cindy said as the boat stuck fast against the mud bank and the man took hold of the rope.

"I could ask you the same thing," he retorted. "Ain't you kinda old to have a sweetie, Unk?"

"I'm his granddaughter!" Cindy said indignantly.

"Granddaughter!" The man, who was about her own age, squinted at her. "Whose girl are you?"

"I'm Cindy Sharp, Martha's daughter."

He studied her some more, then broke into a laugh. "Well, I guess that makes us cousins, kind of. I'm Joe's boy, Calvin. Old Nick's my great-uncle."

"Is that true, Grandpa?"

"This man is an angel of Lucifer," said her grandfather. Then he sighed. "He's my brother's grandson. And he's no good. But I guess we're all God's chirrun."

"What's he talking about?" said Calvin.

Cindy ignored his question. "Well, if you don't mind, we're going to get out here and stretch our legs." But she made no attempt to move.

"How'd you find me?" Nick asked.

"It was easy to figure you out, old man," Calvin said. "I found your campsite on Red Creek, saw where you'd packed up and left. Thought you'd shake me, huh?"

"What is this all about?" Cindy demanded.

"I knew all I had to do was get to the next bridge here before you did and wait," Calvin continued. "It was a long way around, but I made it all right. Wasn't hard to do with that fancy red sports car."

"What sports car?" Cindy was suddenly alarmed.

"Oh, is that yours?" He chuckled. "Nice little car. You didn't have enough gas in it, though. I run out about a mile up the road. Had to leave it and walk."

"You stole my car?" Furious, she stepped out of the boat, fists clenched.

He raised the shotgun. "You just calm down. And get back in that boat. Old man, you move up, get in the middle."

"What's going on here?" Cindy said.

"You just do what I say." His voice had acquired a chilling tone, and she intuitively obeyed.

The man climbed into the stern of the boat, made unwieldy by his added weight. He kept his gun trained on their backs as Cindy took her place in the bow and Nick settled down in the middle.

"Come on, let's go," the man ordered. "We'll talk about it when we get out on the river. Move!"

Cindy pushed off with her paddle.

CHAPTER 15

When Cindy saw a sandbar, white and long, on the right side of the river a mile below the bridge, she felt betrayed. Thanks to her grandfather's delusions, she had begun to think of their drama in terms of divine intervention.

She had hoped that lack of a camping place would force this Calvin person to turn back. The sandbar could only serve to prolong their plight, perhaps even worsen it. She had no idea what the man wanted, but she didn't trust him a bit.

After they dragged the boat up onto the sand, Cindy pitched her tent, her grandfather strung his tarpaulin, and Calvin built a campfire. It might have been a family outing were it not for the shotgun cradled under the intruder's arm.

Cindy fried catfish over the fire. No mention was made of setting out lines, and no one spoke as they ate. When they finished, Calvin pulled a half-empty pint of whiskey from his back pocket and took a big slug.

"This is it," he said, holding up the bottle against

the firelight. "This is all I got left in the world—thanks to you." He motioned to Nick.

"What did he do to you?" Cindy said in a low voice.

Calvin laughed harshly. "What did he do? Got me thrown in jail, that's what. Messed my life up for sure. Ain't that right, Unk?"

Nick stood up and moved off to his lean-to.

"Hey, where you going?" Calvin called after him, but the old man made no answer, disappearing into the darkness of his shelter.

Mist crept off the river, obscuring the stars. Mosquitoes buzzed around Cindy's ears.

"What are you going to do with us?" she asked.

"I'm just along for the ride. I lost my wheels, got no place to go. Thought I'd go fishing, too." The whiskey was disappearing fast. "Hey, if you're my cousin, how come I never seen you before?"

"I lived in Philadelphia most of my life," Cindy said. "We just moved back here a couple years ago."

"Philadelphia, Mississippi, or up north?"

"Pennsylvania," she muttered. She rolled her sleeves down and buttoned them to keep the mosquitoes off.

"So you left the big city to come to Mississippi? You ain't got no sense, girl."

"I came with my mother. Besides, I like Mississippi."

"You like Mississippi? Hooo! You are dumb, or crazy." He drained the bottle and threw it toward the river, where it landed with a plunk. The gun lay between his knees, its barrel pushed carelessly into the sand. "Me, I just want to get out of Mississippi."

Cindy could see that so much whiskey so fast had made him tipsy. She wondered if she should try to catch him off-guard and grab the gun. She wasn't sure he was truly dangerous. He hadn't threatened them, exactly, she reflected. But what if he got worse?

"You plan to stay here?" he said. "You got a job or something?"

"I'm going to school, at Southern. When I get out—I don't know—I may get a job in Hattiesburg, or I may go to Jackson."

With one part of her mind she was trying to maintain this absurdly casual conversation, while with another part she was plotting. She was afraid to try anything with him awake. He looked strong and mean.

"What about you?" she asked.

"I'd like to go to Florida. The fast life, the good life. Plenty of chicks and dope. Mississippi's too small for me, babe. I need somewhere fast, like Pensacola or Miami. Yeah, Miami. That's the place for me."

"I'm afraid our boat won't get us to Miami."

He looked at her strangely. "Where's the old man keep his money?"

"What money?"

He cursed. "What money? You know what money! That old man is loaded with bread, or don't you know it? Yeah, you with your little-girl act. You ain't fooling no one, sister." He stared hard at her, then relaxed.

"Ever seen them murder mysteries on TV?" he asked. "Well, what we got here is a mystery.

Where's the bread? Where's the jack? The sooner we find that, the sooner this show will come to an end."

"If that's all you want, it should be easy to figure out," she said, suddenly hopeful. If he found money, maybe he'd leave them be. "Just search our gear. If he has any money, I don't know about it. But maybe he does. Did you look in the duffel bag?"

"No, but don't think I won't."

He raised the gun suddenly, sighting down the black barrel at the river as though he'd spotted prey. Cindy shivered.

He lowered the gun. "Don't think I'm stupid, cousin Cindy. Forget your lousy sister tricks. You and that old man. Yeah. Uh-huh. Where do you keep the whiskey?"

"We don't have any. He quit drinking."

"Lying woman!" The suddenness of his rage made her flinch. "He's drunk all his life. I'm sick of your lies. No whiskey, no money."

She tried to remain calm. "He got kicked in the head by a mule, and after that he started talking about Jesus and reading his Bible. It surprised me too. But he quit drinking, even quit playing blues. Seriously. Now all he'll play is spirituals."

"Kicked by a mule, huh?"

"Yes. Did you know about it?"

"That what he said? A mule?" Calvin seemed amused.

"Yes. Why?"

He shook his head. "I guess being kicked by a mule's enough to convert anybody."

Now that his anger had passed she was shaking. "I think I'll turn in," she said.

He looked at the fire, nodding slightly. She rose, brushed the sand off her jeans, and went to her tent.

———

The sound of the door unzipping woke her suddenly. She sat up in alarm as Calvin climbed through the opening.

"What are you doing?" she demanded.

"Calm down. The mosquitoes are eating me, that's all."

She backed away from him.

"Be cool, sister. I ain't gonna hurt you. We're kin, remember?"

"I'm going out."

"Silly woman. I don't care."

She crawled out of the tent in a hurry, zipping it behind her.

The moon was up; its light silvered the river and lay like frost on the sand. The fire had burned down to coals. A body-length depression in the sand showed where Calvin had stretched out by the fire. She put a few sticks on and poked up the blaze. Mosquitoes honed in on her. She slapped at them, then rummaged through the dew-soaked duffel bag for mosquito repellent and sprayed herself down.

It was chilly in the mist, and she pulled on a jacket. She remembered lying in the tent, plotting uselessly, before sleep swept it all aside and claimed her. Too much exertion, too many worries that day had exhausted her. Now she felt groggy and confused.

As she built up the fire she realized she was in a position of advantage. Calvin was inside; she was out. He would be sleeping soon, if not already. She pondered the alternatives.

She could waken her grandfather and they could try to sneak away in the boat. That would be tricky, with all the movement and noise. They'd have to get well away before Calvin woke up or he might shoot.

She could set out alone on foot and go for help. She felt certain she could steal away unnoticed. But where to? A wall of thick brush hemmed the sandbar, dense willow thickets backed by cypress swamp. She'd likely get lost. She could try to follow the riverbank, swimming when necessary, but the thought of muddy water, snakes, and alligators made her shudder.

Another alternative appealed to her. Take the boat alone. Alone she could quietly maneuver into the river and paddle downstream. The first bridge or house she came to, she would get help. Or it might be better to paddle back upriver to the bridge they'd already passed. After all, she knew it was there, and there was no telling how far she would have to go downstream to find help.

If she did that, she at least had to tell her grandfather so he wouldn't worry. She walked to the side of the tent. From the sound of Calvin's breathing she knew he was asleep. She crept to the lean-to, where the old man lay wrapped in a blanket. She knelt beside him and shook his shoulder gently.

"Grandpa," she whispered. "Grandpa."

He moaned and rolled over. "Effie?"

Cindy froze, certain the sound of his voice would give them away. He mumbled something else, and then his breathing resumed the rhythm of slumber.

She left him and stopped at the tent again. Calvin hadn't stirred.

Barefoot, for her shoes were in the tent, she made her way to the boat, which lay several yards from the water's edge. Gingerly she slid it toward the water, cringing at the sound of metal against sand. She stopped and waited. Nothing. She took a deep breath and slid it completely out. Done. She climbed in, took a paddle, and shoved off with silent strokes.

The boat glided effortlessly toward the middle of the river. She looked back to the sandbar and, reassured, turned upstream. Strangely, the boat wallowed heavily. With a gasp of alarm, she felt cold water flooding around her feet. She paddled fiercely, baffled, not sure even which way to go—back ashore, across the river, or upstream. When water sloshed around her ankles, she knew there was no hope. She headed back to the sandbar, fighting hard with the paddle. By the time she reached shallow water, the boat was half full. She jumped out and pulled the boat alongside her in the water as she waded ashore.

When she looked up, she saw Calvin standing at the water's edge, watching with amusement, the gun under one arm. "What's a matter? Forget something?"

As she dragged the vessel onto the sand and emptied it, he held up the boat plug. "This what you looking for?" He chuckled. "Going for a midnight ride, cousin? Going fishing maybe? Gonna catch our breakfast?"

"Oh, shut up."

96

"Stupid chick." His humor was gone. "Now I'm go'n have to tie you."

He unfastened the rope from the boat and grabbed Cindy's elbow, shoving her toward the campfire. She jerked away, angry but afraid. Setting the gun down, Calvin pulled her arms behind her and wrapped the rope tightly around her wrists. He pushed her down, and she fell with a grunt in the sand. He yanked her feet up behind her, hog-tying her. He seemed to grow increasingly furious as he worked; she could hear his irregular breathing.

"Stupid chick," he repeated. "You ain't go'n get away from Calvin. Now I know you got it all—money, whiskey, you probably even got coke, huh sugar?"

Seeing her terror, Calvin relaxed and chuckled. He stroked her cheek with his left hand. With a sudden movement he drew a knife from his pocket and opened it, leaning in close to her. He grabbed her hair and pulled her head back viciously, laying the blade tightly against her throat.

"Just try me," he said low, panting. "Just try me, babe. You want to try me? Huh? Huh?"

She tried to shake her head, but he held it firmly, straining her neck, pulling her hair. "No," she grunted. He yanked her head back harder.

"Don't make me do it," he breathed, and she knew she had underestimated him. He was a killer, a psycho. She should have fled on foot. No matter how bad the swamp, it couldn't be worse than this.

He held the blade in front of her face. A drop of blood from her neck beaded on its edge, glimmering in the firelight.

"I like it," he murmured intimately, confessionally. "You know?"

She couldn't answer. He let her go and sat back. She lay helpless on her side, uncomfortably tethered.

He blinked, and she could see that he was sleepy, exhausted after his outburst of madness. He slapped a mosquito and stretched out beside her.

"Relax. You ain't hurt," he said, and closed his eyes, licked his lips, and slept.

CHAPTER 16

Cindy opened her eyes to gray light. She had drifted in and out of a nightmare awareness with brief intervals of rain-washed peace. Those moments lasted only until her uncomfortable position reminded her of her plight.

Calvin lay asleep beside her in the sand, mouth open. She heard a sound and tilted her head back.

Her grandfather stood at Calvin's head holding the shotgun, looking relaxed and patient. He smiled at her.

"You all right, honey?"

She nodded, amazed and relieved.

Calvin stirred and opened his eyes. Sensing a presence behind him, he jumped to his feet.

Nick stepped back and raised the gun to his shoulder warningly. "Hold it!"

"Hey, old man, what you doing?" Calvin glanced to either side, frightened, confused, conniving. He chuckled nervously. "What's happening, cousin?" Suddenly he lunged.

Nick pulled the trigger, but the sound that followed wasn't what Cindy expected. It was a hollow thunder, and her grandfather immediately dropped the gun and put his hands to his eyes. She looked at the fallen weapon, smoke streaming from its shattered breech, and she remembered Calvin absent-mindedly shoving the barrel into the sand.

"Grandpa!" she cried as she saw blood pour between his fingers. He made a whimpering sound and sank down in the sand.

Calvin stood staring, slowly figuring out what had happened. Then he laughed harshly. "You old fool!" He picked up the twisted metal and examined it. "Won't you people ever learn?" He hurled the gun into the river.

"He's hurt!" Cindy said, struggling against her bonds.

"Ain't he though. Here, let me see, Unk." Calvin knelt and pried Nick's fingers away from his face. He inhaled sharply at the sight.

"Water," Nick said. "Get me to the water."

"Calvin, untie me! Let me help!"

He cut her free. Ignoring her stiff joints, she hurried to her grandfather and led him to the river's edge. Stumbling, he fell to all fours and began splashing handfuls of water onto his face. When she caught a glimpse of his wounds, she turned away with a gasp.

"You!" she shouted at Calvin, who approached almost guiltily. "See what you've done!"

"Me? He's the one that tried to shoot me."

"What'd you expect after what you did?" she yelled. "We've got to get him to a doctor."

"Just a minute, now, just a minute. Here, let me see." He looked closely at Nick's face, streaming

100

with blood and water. Both eyes and the bridge of his nose were a mangled mass.

Cindy ran to her duffel bag and pulled out a shirt. She ripped a long strip from it, soaked it in the river, and bound it around Nick's face.

"You're going to be all right, Grandpa," she said. "We'll get you to a doctor now."

Nick just shook his head and moaned, putting his hands to the bandage that was already soaked with blood. Cindy led him to the lean-to and made him lie back on the blanket.

"Lie still and let the bleeding stop," she told him. "It'll be okay."

He grabbed at her. "Cindy, Cindy baby." He sounded like he was crying.

"Grandpa, it's all right." If not for the terror inhabiting her bones, she would have pressed her head against his shoulder and wept herself.

He shook his head. "My Bible. I won't be able to read my Bible."

"Sure you will. We'll take you to a doctor and he'll fix you up like new."

He continued to shake his head. "Will you read to me, Cindy baby?"

"Of course I will. You just rest now."

When she backed out of the lean-to and turned toward the water, she saw Calvin screwing the plug in the boat.

"We're going to have to paddle up to the bridge," she told him. "Get to a phone and call an ambulance."

He looked around, and his merciless eyes chilled

her to the bone. "No we ain't. We going down-stream."

"No! Calvin, no."

"Oh yeah. Come on, get your stuff ready."

"What about Grandpa?"

"We're taking him too. Come on, hurry up."

She considered making a stand. He had no gun now; maybe she could handle him. But she remembered the knife and, more importantly, his capacity for irrational violence. So she turned to break camp.

Once they had loaded the boat, they set out on the river—Calvin in the stern, Nick in the middle gripping both sides of the boat, Cindy in front. The overloaded vessel rode low in the water.

"Where are we going?" Cindy asked after they had paddled awhile.

"Don't you worry about it, cousin. Just keep stroking." Calvin ordered.

"Are you all right, Grandpa?" She turned to the old man, but Calvin slammed his paddle against the side of the boat, startling her.

"I said paddle! He's all right."

She turned away and dipped the blade in the cold brown river.

CHAPTER 17

They paddled all day, pausing only briefly to eat lunch on a mud flat. The heavily loaded flatbottom boat made slow progress in the dawdling current.

Nick seemed to have sunk into a state of semi-consciousness, slumped forward, groaning quietly from time to time.

"Listen!" Calvin said suddenly as they drifted down a wide stretch of river in the late afternoon.

Cindy heard the sound of an approaching motorboat, and her heart began to beat with hope.

"Over there," Calvin said, pointing to a narrow channel to their left, flowing out of the cypress woods. "Come on, hurry."

He steered the boat around until it was headed for the inlet, then began to paddle hard, but Cindy was slow to join. He slammed the side of the boat. "Don't make me get ugly, cousin!" he said. "Move it." She began to stroke.

As they entered the slough, the bushes closed behind them and she heard the motorboat cruise by at open throttle on the river.

"Perfect," Calvin said when it was gone. "Come on, keep going. I want to see where this leads."

Limbs arched overhead, casting them in eerie shadow. The channel wound among trunks and cypress knees before emerging into a narrow lake.

"Dead river," Calvin said. "I like the looks of this place."

They drifted slowly across the lake, disturbing a great blue heron which hoisted its graceful body in sluggish flight and swooped out of sight, following the curve of the lake.

"Let's try over there," Calvin said, indicating a narrow point extended into the lake, covered in cypress trees draped with Spanish moss. "We'll camp there if there's enough solid ground."

Cindy didn't say a word, crushed by the missed chance of help from the passing boat. Events seemed to be shaping into a fatal design, as if their doom was preplanned.

The boat bumped against cypress knees growing around the point, and Cindy climbed out, stepping into the shallows and tugging the boat up onto the land. The place was just wide enough for a tent among the trees. It would be a mosquito-infested campsite, though, she figured.

"This looks good," Calvin said. "Go ahead and set up camp. Then you can cook supper."

Cindy helped her grandfather out of the boat and led him to a tree to sit down. He leaned against it for support. Then she pitched the tent and strung the lean-to while Calvin managed to get a fire going with some soggy wood. She fried catfish for supper. Nick wouldn't eat, though they propped him against the ice chest in front of the fire, nor would he respond to her solicitations.

Mosquitoes came out in force with the dusk, and they applied repellent and threw damp moss onto the fire to smoke them away.

"I like this," Calvin said in a relaxed voice, settling back. "Nice and cozy."

The fire burned low, throwing off as much steam as smoke, giving the air a woodsy flavor and hemming them in close on this small strip of land, while the stars struggled to make their presence known through the heavy mist and bullfrogs bellowed like thunder. Nick was silent, and Cindy could not tell if he was conscious under his bandage. Wrapped inside herself, she listened to the night sounds: the hiss and crackle of the fire, the crowded rhythms of frogs and insects, the lonely cries of an owl, and the chirps and moans of creatures unknown.

"You know, I ain't such a bad dude," Calvin said. "Hope I haven't given you the wrong impression."

Cindy said nothing.

"We ain't that close a cousin," he went on. "Second or third maybe. Right?"

"I don't know."

"What do you do for fun, Cindy? How do you spend your Saturday nights?"

She merely shrugged.

"You don't have to be so stuck up."

He stood up and dragged a thick cypress limb to the fire. He laid the end of it in the flames, where it smoldered and slowly began to blaze. Nick propped a foot against it, his first sign of life.

105

"What about it, Unk?" Calvin slapped Nick's leg as he sat down. "Feeling better? How's them eyes, huh?"

When the old man didn't answer, Calvin stared at him, then nodded. "I got it," he said. "I think I'm finally getting it figured out. He's senile, right? Addle-brained? That it, cousin? That what you meant by all his Jesus stuff?" He nodded again and poked Nick. "Where's your money? Where do you keep your jack, old-timer?"

"Oh, give it up, Calvin," Cindy said, disgusted.

He looked at her sharply. "Why you telling me what to do? Huh?" He stared at her intently. "Get up."

"What?"

"Get up!"

She jumped to her feet, frightened by his tone.

"That's it. Stand in the light where I can see you. You an all-right looking babe, you know that, Cindy? Even if you are my cousin. Maybe you and me could get it on, huh?"

She forced herself to stare at him evenly. "You'd have to kill me first."

He smiled and looked down, began cleaning his fingernails with his knife. "That right? Suppose I told you to take your shirt off for me?"

"I'd tell you to—"

Calvin sprang to his feet. "How about if I just take it off myself?"

"Keep away." Her voice was low and scared.

He approached. "Aw, Cindy." He put one hand on her shoulder and held the knife in front of her face.

Orange sparks rose behind him as though the fire had flared to life. Cindy flinched just as Nick slammed the blazing end of the limb down on Calvin's shoulder, driving him to his knees.

She jumped out of the way as her grandfather swung the flaming end again, like a baseball bat, at Calvin's head. He missed and almost lost his balance. Dazed, the younger man struggled to get up, and Nick swung again. Burning embers broke loose from the impact, falling down Calvin's shirt. The fabric flickered to life and he screamed, wiping at his face with one hand and swatting his shirt with the other.

Guided by the screams, Nick brought the limb down on his head, as though knighting him, and a halo took shape. It took Cindy a moment to realize Calvin's hair had caught fire. He turned toward the water in a howling panic as Nick rammed the end of the limb into his body. His hands and sleeves blazing from the sticky polyester flame of his shirt, Calvin clawed at himself as he plummeted, his cries swallowed abruptly by the water.

He came up once, gasping, a steaming charcoal figure of a man, and then went under. The water roiled gently and slowly grew still.

Appalled by the swiftness of it all, Cindy stood in the ankle-deep water where she had stumbled when she moved aside. Nick turned blindly in her direction, dropping the branch in the lake. It sizzled and went out.

"Cindy?"

"Yes. Here, Grandpa." Her voice trembled. She resisted the urge to run to him.

"You all right, girl?"

"Yes. I'm okay."

He tilted his head back as if straining to pinpoint her location. Then he relaxed.

Cindy couldn't relax. Several times she left the cozy circle of firelight to peer out at the lake. Its surface remained undisturbed. She had changed Nick's bandage, replacing it with a fresh strip of cloth and dabbing water on his awful wound. Now he sat in front of the fire, seemingly content, as if he could see its low blaze.

"You know, the mind is a wondrous thing," he said finally. "I been pond'ring what little bit I've read in the Bible, and you know what? I can remember it just like I was looking at it."

"That's wonderful, Grandpa," she said weakly, alternately staring at the blaze and glancing out into the darkness.

"And you know what I remembered while I was sitting here a while ago? I remembered when Samson was blind and captured. And Samson called on the Lord and said, 'O Lord, remember me, I pray thee, and strengthen me.'" He paused. "That's somewhere in Judges. God answers our prayers, sugar, don't you doubt it."

"Yes, Grandpa."

Somehow his words soothed her. She settled back against a log and stretched her legs out. Her jeans were incredibly filthy; mosquitoes danced along the dark folds of denim.

"Sing me a song, Grandpa."

He smiled, leaning against the ice chest. Then he began to sing in a low voice:

"I've got these blues, means I'm not satisfied,
I've got these blues, I'm not satisfied,
That's the reason why I stole away and cried.

"Blues grabbed me at midnight, didn't turn me
    loose till day,
Blues grabbed me at midnight, didn't turn me
    loose till day,
I didn't have no mama to drive these blues away.

"The big star fallin', mama 'tain't long for day,
The big star fallin', mama 'tain't long for day,
Maybe the sunshine will drive these blues away."

When he finished, tears were running down her face.

"That's an old blues song," he said. "I remembered how you like the blues."

She sniffed, brushing the tears away with her shirt sleeve.

"Blues ain't necessarily bad," he went on. "I guess it's what kind of blues, how you sing 'em. I don't know. I never read nothing about blues in the Good Book."

"There's nothing wrong with the blues you sing, Grandpa."

A dull thought stirred in her brain. "Who wrote that song, do you know?" she asked. "Wasn't that by Blind Willie McTell?"

"Blind Willie who?"

"McTell."

He shook his head. "I don't know. May be. Tonight it's by Blind Nick Rose."

She leaned over and kissed his grizzled cheek. "That's good enough for me."

CHAPTER 18

Unable to stay awake any longer, Cindy helped her grandfather into the tent and stretched out beside him on her sleeping bag. Despite a nagging sense of unease, she fell asleep instantly.

Deep in the night she sat up suddenly, eyes wide though she was not fully awake. The lake had risen, the water was about to flood their tent. Through the mosquito netting she could see water all around.

She unzipped the door and stuck her hand out, but the ground was as dry as ever, the night still and peaceful. Feeling crowds of mosquitoes cluster on her hand, she shook them off and jerked back, zipping the door quickly. Then she lay back and slept again.

When the dead gray light of dawn infiltrated the mist imprisoning their spit of land, she woke to the sound of snapping wood. Through the gauzy tent door she saw her grandfather sitting by the fire, his back to her.

Only when she was halfway out of the tent did she notice that the old man was still asleep inside.

The figure by the fire turned slowly to face her,

and her blood froze in pure acid fear. For an instant she believed—she wished—she was back in her nightmare.

Calvin's face was hideously disfigured from his burns—one eye swollen shut, clumps of hair singed off. His shirt clung to him in shreds, melted onto his skin like plastic.

She tried to scream but her voice was locked tight.

He smiled at her. "Morning, cousin."

Somehow she mustered a surge of willpower and stepped out of the tent.

"Calvin!" she half-whispered, as much in pity as in shock.

"Done a job on me, didn't you?" His grin was vast. "You and the old man." His voice sounded incongruously cordial.

Nick stirred inside the tent. "Cindy baby? What is it?" His bandaged face appeared at the door.

"Howdy, Unk."

Nick did not move. He too seemed trapped in a dream. At last he murmured, "Lord Jesus."

"It's all right, Grandpa," Cindy said uncertainly.

"Yeah, it's all right," Calvin said. "Come on out and have breakfast. We're all family here, ain't we?"

Cindy grabbed a stick and wielded it like a baseball bat.

Calvin only laughed. "I ain't go'n try nothing," he said in a voice devoid of hostility. "Ya'll done took the starch out of me, cousin Cindy."

"If you try anything, so help me, I'll—"

He turned back to the fire. Presented with the back of his head, she automatically tightened her grip on

112

the wood and stepped forward. Calvin poked at the fire.

Pausing behind him, she raised the stick tentatively. At that instant Calvin wheeled, throwing a handful of ashes into her face, and tackled her solidly. They wrestled for a moment, grunting, before he subdued her. His marred face stared at her, inches away.

"I said I wasn't going to hurt you. Don't you believe me?" he said fiercely.

She smelled the stench of his burned flesh. His right eye was seared and swollen shut, and milky liquid seeped from his left, leaving a trail down his cheek. His lips were grayish white.

"Huh? Don't you believe me?" he demanded.

"Y–yes," she managed.

He let her up and returned to the fire, sitting down with his back to her once more.

"Now leave me alone, you hear me?" he said.

Puzzled and shaken, she picked herself up.

"Cindy," her grandfather called.

She helped him out of the tent and settled him on a log by the crackling fire.

"Fix us some breakfast, will you, Cindy?" Calvin said in a neutral voice.

"What happened, boy?" Nick inquired matter-of-factly.

"Like I told her, you two did a number on me, you sure did," Calvin said.

"I thought you was dead," Nick murmured.

"This is the last of the fish," Cindy said, bending over the open ice chest. "The ice is all melted."

"I thought I was dead too," Calvin said. "I went

under, and when I come up I didn't know where I was or who I was. I crawled up in the mud and went away from here." He tapped his head. "Now I'm almost as bad off as you are, Unk. My right eye's near-about gone." He sounded pitiful.

"I'm sorry about that, nephew," Nick said, his words surprising Cindy. She spread the coals out and set a skillet over them, pouring oil into it. "I didn't have any choice. You was messing with Cindy."

Calvin nodded. "You right. You right. I don't hold no grudges."

Cindy stared at Calvin in angry disbelief. Yet he seemed sincere—or, more likely, delirious.

"When it got daylight I looked around and seen the tent and everything over here," he said. "I wasn't but a little ways off. Right over there." He pointed to the woods a short distance across the lake. "I said here goes nothing and swum for it."

"Calvin, what's come over you?" Cindy demanded skeptically.

He chuckled again, shaking his head. "I don't know. It's like I been—cleansed or something."

"Praise Jesus!" Nick said, raising his hands and turning his face to the fog-choked dawn sky. "He's done been buried and resurrected, just like our Lord. Give me your hand, boy."

"What?"

"Give me your hand. That's it. Feel the life in you, boy. You done casted off your evil husk. You're reborn, like me. Feel it?"

Calvin frowned. "Feel what, Unk?"

"The power of Jesus, boy! Don't you see? That's

why you was saved. You was dead, and now you're reborn. And you got Jesus to thank for that."

Calvin pulled his hand away and nodded. "I guess you're right, Uncle Nick. That must be what saved me. I hadn't thought of it."

"The Lord works in mysterious ways his wonders to perform," Nick recited. "Hear that, Cindy? Your cousin has seen the light, just like I did. When you hit me, Calvin, that's when it happened for me. I was falling straight down into the fiery furnace, and something caught me, and I opened my eyes and seen this pure white light with the cross of Jesus right there in it. And now I hit you in the head and you've seen the light." He slapped his leg and cackled. "Did you see a cross, Calvin?"

"Can't say as I did."

"Well, it's different for everybody, I reckon."

Grease sizzled as Cindy lay strips of battered fish into the skillet. She frowned at their insane conversation.

"Just goes to show Jesus can help anybody—even me and Calvin," Nick went on.

"Oh, Grandpa!" Cindy exclaimed. "Can't you see he's leading you on? Calvin doesn't have Jesus or anything else except pure conniving hatred. Isn't that right, Calvin?"

Calvin grinned, shrugged, and held both hands palm up. "I don't know what I got, cousin Cindy. I don't see what you're fired up about anyway. You got what you wanted. You took care of me. Look at me. Look at me!" He began to shake with sobs. "You done for me good. Ain't you happy now?"

Cindy touched Calvin's shoulder, amazing even

herself. "It's all right," she said. "We'll get out of here and all be all right."

"Praise Jesus!" Nick exulted.

A hoot owl answered, its lunatic voice echoing over the water. Cindy turned back to the frying fish, her eyes stinging from the smoke.

CHAPTER 19

After they'd eaten and packed up, they made their way back to the main river, where they drifted lazily, too exhausted to put much effort into paddling. Calvin had not even argued when Cindy had taken the stern position, had not even objected when she suggested paddling upstream to the bridge. It was Nick who talked her out of that, saying it would be too much work to go against the current, that they should float down to the next town or bridge.

Cindy was convinced now that Calvin was truly in her power. He had not been lying when he said his suffering had taken the starch out of him. Plus, she was certain he no longer even had his knife; she had checked for that, examining the outline of his pockets carefully. Even if his old persona emerged, she could handle him with a boat paddle and her dauntless determination.

As they floated, dipping a paddle now and then, Nick began preaching to Calvin about the joys of the Christian life.

"I don't know what your pa told you about me, but I was as evil a man as walked the country when I was young," Nick said, gripping the gunwales on either side of him, staring blindly ahead as if lecturing the river.

"I was every bit as evil as you, Calvin, boy. Never kilt a man, but it weren't for lack of trying. I cut a man once—" he laughed ruminatively at the memory. "Cindy, I didn't want you to know all this, but it's probably better that you do. It just goes to show the power of the Lord. He done raised me up. Calvin, I cut a man once from here to here." He gestured across his side and belly. "His guts was hanging half out. If it wasn't for old Dr. Werner, he'd a been dead sho'. Doc Werner was handy with a needle, always sewing up the sawhands when they cut themselves."

Cindy sighed. Though her position was infinitely better than it had been the day before, she was still in the middle of a swamp with two crazy men, both in dire need of medical help.

She heard a boat motoring their way and wondered for a moment if Calvin would try anything, but he didn't make a move as the boat rounded a bend and came into sight, throttling down as it approached. It contained an older man with a crew cut and a young man with a wad of snuff in his lower lip.

"Howdy," said the older man with a cautionary smile.

"Ya'll catching anything?" said the younger.

Both frowned when they spotted Nick's bloody bandage and Calvin's awful burns.

"We've had a little accident," Cindy told them. "Can you tell us where the nearest town is?"

The men exchanged glances. "There's Three Rivers Landing," said the older man. "But it's a long ways from here. Is there something we can do to help?"

Cindy thought fast. "No," she said. "We can make it all right."

The men exchanged glances again.

"We're okay, really," she said, not sure why she was reluctant to ask for help. Maybe she felt safe now and didn't want to cause a fuss. Maybe she wanted to get out under her own power. "Is Three Rivers Landing on this river?"

"Yes'm. On the east bank."

"About how far?"

The older man shrugged. "It'll take you a while in that thing."

"Can I get there before dark?"

The younger man glanced at his friend questioningly, then nodded. "I don't see any reason why not. Are you sure we can't help you out somehow?"

"I'm sure," she said determinedly.

They nodded uncertainly, then motored on.

Calvin turned and looked at Cindy, his face almost clownish in its disfigurement. "Thanks."

She looked away, frowning.

———

The sky began to cloud up before noon. "We'd better take a break," Cindy said. "It's about lunchtime anyway."

"We got anything to eat?" Calvin asked.

"There's some bread."

"I ain't seen a sandbar for a long time."

"Well, let's stop at the next place that looks like anything."

Nick had not spoken for some time. Leaning forward in his seat, apparently asleep, he seemed to have played out. Calvin too sat with the air of a broken, exhausted man. The relief Cindy felt at his meekness was offset by her burden of responsibility for both men. Strangely, she harbored no hostility toward Calvin, even after all he had done. She pitied him.

Rain had begun to peck around them when she spotted a narrow mud flat scarcely above water level. "This will do," she said, clearly in command.

She and Calvin angled the boat ashore. Just as they stepped out, a downpour deluged them.

"Let's get the tent up, quick!" she yelled, racing across the mud flat. Calvin followed, and they wrestled with the tent while Nick sat hunched over in the boat, oblivious to everything.

When the tent was in place, Calvin climbed inside while Cindy went for Nick. She led him, drenched and shivering, across to the shelter and bundled him in. They closed all the flaps to keep out the driving rain and huddled inside, clothes wet and teeth chattering. Water running off them pooled onto the fabric floor.

"All our gear is getting wet!" Cindy lamented.

"It's all right," Nick muttered to no one in particular. He curled up onto his side, shivering.

"Oh, Grandpa," she said, lying against him and wrapping her arms around him to share her body heat. She berated herself now for not getting the two fishermen to help. Foolish pride!

She heard Calvin stretch out behind her. Looking around, she saw him lying on his side with his back to her. She shook her head, as bewildered by his strange complacency as by the whole, odd series of events.

She inched closer to her grandfather and fell asleep.

A rustling sound outside the tent made Cindy open her eyes. Someone unzipped the cloth door, revealing a pair of muddy rubber boots. Slowly the person dropped to her level in a squat—a white, grizzled backwoodsman cradling a rifle. He peered in at her and the two men slumbering on either side of her.

Lying on her back, head raised, Cindy watched as the man grinned at her, his toothless gums brown with tobacco juice. Uncradling his rifle, he turned it around and inserted the muzzle into his own mouth. Never dropping his gaze, he reached down the gun's scarred wooden forearm and found the trigger with the side of his thumb.

"No," she breathed.

He applied pressure.

She sat upright in panic, her heart racing. The door was zipped tight. Rain pattered the fabric.

She opened the door to make sure she had only been dreaming and discovered the rustling sound came from muddy, foamy water slathering around the tent, rising quickly.

"Calvin! Grandpa! Wake up! It's flooding!"

"Huh?" Calvin sat up. Nick barely stirred.

As soon as he saw the water surrounding the tent, Calvin dashed outside.

"The boat's gone!" he bellowed.

She hurried out and saw brown water surging down the river, covering the mud flat and threatening to sweep their tent away. The boat was nowhere to be seen.

"Grandpa!" She reached inside and shook him fiercely. "Come on!" She grabbed his collar and pulled him out. He stood up, bewildered, groping. Calvin was already headed for the willow thicket bordering the river.

"Run, Grandpa. Follow me!" Holding his hand, she raced through ankle-deep water toward the bushes.

Though above the flood, the thicket provided scant refuge. The solid mass of limbs and leaves was heavy with rain, dense with briars, and screaming with mosquitoes. She followed the direction Calvin had taken, struggling to keep hold of her grandfather's hand as she beat her way through the bushes.

The mud sucked at her feet and ankles; bushes whipped her face with the stinging violence of a personal assault. Briars grabbed her blouse and snagged her jeans. One tennis shoe came off in the muck. When she stopped to retrieve it, Nick bumped into her and they both went sprawling.

Lying on her face in the mud, rain hammering her back, mosquitoes pecking her skin, Cindy began to laugh, then cry.

"Calvin!" she shouted, her voice breaking.

She felt certain he had abandoned them, but he

suddenly appeared over her, grabbed them both and yanked them to their feet.

"Come on," he said. "It's better up ahead."

"My shoe!" she wailed. She took a step and slipped again, falling. Her other shoe came off. She reached for it, grabbed it, then in a fit of anger hurled it away.

Nick was laughing. "It's all right," he said. "An angel led us here. The third of the rivers, remember?"

She groaned and, getting to her feet, pulled him along. A short way through the thicket the ground sloped down to an inundated cypress forest where Calvin stood knee-deep in a swamp lake, its surface pocked by rain.

Cindy stared in astonishment. "You call this better?"

"At least it beats them briars." He scrutinized her and laughed. "You a sight, cousin."

She glanced down. She was a mud-caked scarecrow, a ragamuffin in clay. Her jeans were completely coated, her blouse tattered, sleeves stained red in spots from briar cuts. But Calvin appeared every bit as awful as she did, more so with his Cyclops face. She joined his laughter, hysterically.

"I told you," Nick said happily. "I told you."

Cindy had no idea what he meant. Mustering her courage, she plunged into the water, immersing herself. She came up blowing.

"That's better," she said. "But cold!"

Grinning, Calvin shook his head and set off through the swamp.

"Wait!" Cindy said. "Shouldn't we go look for the boat?"

"Boat? That boat's in the Gulf of Mexico by now," Calvin said. "We need to get out of this place. It gives me the creeps."

As quickly as their fit of laughter had come on, fear possessed them.

"You reckon there's any gators in this swamp?" Calvin whispered over his shoulder, pausing.

Cindy shivered. "If there are, we're trapped."

"Come on," Nick said. Though blind, he took the lead, wading out into the flooded forest.

Calvin shrugged and fell into place behind him.

Knowing Nick could not stay in the lead, Cindy mustered her resolve and scampered ahead, wading she knew not where.

CHAPTER 20

She stopped when the cold water reached her armpits.

"What do we do now?" she wailed, feeling she had reached her limit at last. The swamp lake had deepened gradually, spreading in every direction. "It's going to be over our heads if we keep going this way."

"You wait here," Calvin said. "I'll check it out."

"Hurry!" she said, shivering, as he waded off. Alligators, snakes, leeches, snapping turtles—who knew what lurked underneath this deep water?

Nick stood behind her, patient and mute. "Oh, Grandpa," she said, putting her arms on his shoulders and resting her head against him.

"It's going to be all right, child," he said with a smile. She realized that he had no fear. Perhaps he was delirious.

He began to sing softly:

> "I'm moving up the king's highway,
> I'm moving up the king's highway,
> Satan's on my track and he's trying to

125

turn me back,
But I'm moving up the king's highway."

Cindy closed her eyes gratefully, longing for that age of innocence when she had sat on his front porch while he sang and played.

"Grandpa, I'm freezing," she said so softly that, with his singing, she felt sure he did not hear. "I'm lost and I don't know what to do, Grandpa. If something happens to you it will be all my fault."

After awhile she heard Calvin shout. "Over here!"

"He's found something, Grandpa," she said, her energy renewed by hope. "Come on."

"Easy, child," he said as she pulled him along.

Calvin was standing in shallow water as they approached. "There's a creek over here," he said. "Maybe if we follow it we can get out."

He led them to the edge of the lake and through muddy woods to an unpromising, stagnant inlet.

Cindy looked at the sky, trying to gauge the hour. She had no idea what time it might be. Though the rain had stopped, the sky remained overcast.

"This is the creek?" she said doubtfully. "I don't know, Calvin." She felt sapped. Spotting a log, she released her grandfather's hand and sat down, resting her head in her hands.

Sighing, Calvin sat beside her, while Nick stood with his head up, sniffing the air.

"What you whining about, cousin?" Calvin said gruffly. "Least when we get out of here you got something to look forward to. Me, I got prison—if I'm lucky."

Cindy raised her head. "How's your face? Are you hurting?"

"Shoot!" He glared at the brown water before them. "I bet I'm a sight to see, though." He grinned.

"You'll be all right," she said, not believing it herself. "You don't look too bad."

"It hurts for sure. How about you, Unk? Your face hurt? It's killing me!" He laughed. A discordant note in his voice made Cindy peer at him.

"What are you looking at?" Calvin said, catching her glance. "Come on." He stood up. "We ain't got all day. And I sure don't want to spend the night out here."

"If only I had some dry clothes." Cindy sighed and rose. "Come on, Grandpa," she said, taking his hand.

"It'll be all right," the old man murmured, nodding.

They tried walking along the edge of the slough but soon found it easier, due to the slick mud and dense weeds, simply to wade. As they trudged along, the passage became narrower and shallower.

"You see?" Calvin said. "We're getting to high ground."

The waterway petered out, leaving only a muddy track. Caramel-colored mud slimed around their ankles, releasing a foul odor with each step, and they swatted mosquitoes constantly. But soon they faced another stretch of stagnant water, just like the one they had left.

"Oh, *no!*" Cindy moaned, striking her thigh with her fist. "This swamp goes on forever!"

Calvin snorted and plunged ahead.

As they waded into the cold water, walls of dense switch cane growing on either side of the narrow waterway hemmed them in.

"This is a rotten place," Cindy muttered.

"Ain't it fine?" Nick said, grinning.

She shook her head, weary of his addle-brained mouthings. "Grandpa, please!" she chided.

"Fine, fine," he murmured.

Suddenly Calvin danced aside, skipping sideways across the slough. "Look out! Snake!"

Despite herself Cindy shrieked and let go of Nick's hand, splashing toward the wall of switch cane. She turned to see a thick, curving brown body swimming across the top of the water toward the far bank.

Nick did not move. "What kind is it?" he asked.

"Who cares?" Calvin raged. "It's a snake, that's all!"

"Is it mostly brown or is it yeller with stripes?"

"Dark brown, Grandpa, with a big thick head," Cindy answered. "It's gone now."

Nick nodded. "Cottonmouth. Steer clear of them, chirrun. They're p'isonous."

"What do you mean?" Calvin demanded. "I thought all snakes was poisonous."

Cindy laughed, returning to her grandfather's side. "Calvin, you really are a greenhorn when it comes to the woods, aren't you?"

"What you mean?"

Cindy shook her head. "Here, Grandpa and I will lead the way if you're too chicken."

Somehow Calvin's fear had banished her own. She took the lead, with her grandfather close behind. Calvin fell grudgingly into step behind them.

128

"Looky there, cuz," she heard him say.

Glancing ahead to where he was pointing, she saw a log about head high overarching the slough. As she watched, a brown lump atop it uncoiled and a cottonmouth perhaps five feet long dangled down like a thick rope before hitting the water with a plop.

She shuddered, and this time Calvin laughed. "What's the matter, Supergirl? Not scared of a snake, are you?"

But when the snake started swimming their way, both scampered toward the thicket of switchcane, Cindy tugging Nick behind her. "Run, Grandpa, it's chasing us!"

Nick laughed as he picked his way behind her. "It's true," he said. "Cottonmouth'll come after you, I'm telling you."

The snake angled away from them, disappearing in the bushes on the far side.

"Let's sit here a minute," Cindy said, breathing hard. She wedged a place to sit in the muck at the base of the cane stalks.

"Ever been snakebit, old man?" Calvin asked.

"Oh yeah." Nick chuckled. "I was down on Red Creek one time fishing when I reached for the end of my trotline and felt something sting my hand. I drew it back, and there was about a fourteen-inch cottonmouth hanging from my middle finger. It felt like if you was to grab that plug wire on your lawn mower and just hang on. It hurt deep. I flung it loose and it landed in the boat. I busted its head with my boat paddle and got back to camp in a hurry. My old truck wouldn't crank and I was low on whiskey, so I could see there weren't but one thing to do."

"What's that?" Cindy asked in a hushed voice.

"Tough it out. I lay down on the bank and filled my belly with river water."

"Were you very sick?" she asked.

"Sick as I ever been. My arm swole up big as my leg. I tried sucking the p'ison out but that didn't do no good. Along about dawn I fell asleep, and when I woke up I felt a sight better. I laid around that day, and that night I went ahead and run my trotlines."

Calvin looked back to the creek. "I bet if one that big had a got you, you wouldn't a been running no trotline. Huh, Cindy?"

"It was a big one all right," she said.

"Let's go," Calvin said, eyeing the canebrake nervously. "These bushes are liable to be full of snakes."

Cindy stood up quickly, glancing around. "You're right."

"Yep, ain't no better place for snakes than a canebrake," Nick said. "Gators don't mind 'em neither."

Calvin winced. "Now why'd you have to go and remind us of that, old man?"

"If I see a gator in here I think I'll die," Cindy said sincerely.

They eased tentatively up the slough, darting glances about nervously like jungle soldiers. As they rounded a sharp curve—the passage barely three feet wide here, the cane leaves brushing their shoulders—a man-sized shape leapt into the air with a deep croak.

Calvin fell to his belly in the water, hands over his

head. Cindy watched, cringing, as the huge thing took flight, disappearing into the forest.

"It's just a big bird," she told Calvin, who rose sheepishly, dripping wet.

"Great blue heron by the sound of it," Nick said. "Am I right, Cindy?"

"It was big, whatever it was. Tall as a man almost."

Nick nodded. "That's the great blue. Wisest bird in the swamp. Can't nothing sneak up on it, 'cept maybe a gator."

Calvin wheeled angrily. "There you go with that gator talk again! Can't you just shut up about it?"

Nick shrugged.

"Calvin, if this gets any narrower, I don't see how we can follow it," Cindy said.

"Don't look at me, sister. I ain't got no answers."

They edged forward, crouching to avoid the trailing fingers of cane leaves. As the passageway constricted, the high tops met overhead, blocking out the sky, tunneling them in green.

"This don't lead nowhere," Calvin whispered, as if afraid to speak aloud.

"Here, you wait with Grandpa while I go ahead and check it out," Cindy said. Calvin nodded.

She moved nervously, watching for snakes, dipping her head to avoid the spiderwebs that crisscrossed her path. Through the thick green stalks she could see into a world where sunlight never reached the ground, a prison of insects and reptiles.

As the channel turned and twisted, the knee-deep water seemed to grow colder, and she detected a current. Stopping to wipe the sweat off her forehead,

131

she heard a sound like a distant wind. As she continued, she recognized the sound as rushing water. Around the bend the slough narrowed, and she saw a fast-running brook pouring into it through a tight opening in the canebrake. She forced her way through the stalks and, amazingly, before her rose a waterfall, higher than her head, tumbling through a ravine.

She stared in disbelief, gradually realizing she must be standing at the edge of the Pascagoula River bluffs, where cold spring water met stagnant swamp.

She started to turn back to fetch the other two, then decided to investigate the falls herself first. She could use a little time alone.

Approaching gingerly, she put a hand under the clear, clean, icy flow. How could this infernal swamp hold such a heavenly wonder? Such dramatic shifts in terrain must characterize the mysterious wilderness of the Deep South, she reflected. After peering back down the brook to make sure Calvin had not followed her, she stripped and ducked under the bone-chilling cascade, fighting an urge to squeal with pure, childish glee.

Hastened by the coldness of the water, she scrubbed her clothes and herself. Then she wrung out her clothing, the water pattering onto the clay shelf where she stood. A ray of yellow sunlight pierced the clouds and fell through the forest, steaming from the recent rain.

"Thank you, God!" she shouted, laughing as she dressed. She looked up, feeling as secure in his guidance now as Noah must have been at the sight of the rainbow.

As she wedged her way back through the cane-brake, she felt happy, clean, and peaceful. Even the sight of her downtrodden companions could not disturb her mood.

She grinned. "Guess what I found."

"Hooo! You sure prettied up," Calvin said.

Something in his tone made her frown, but she shook it off. "I found a waterfall."

"Waterfall? They ain't no waterfalls in a swamp," Calvin said. "What you think this is, a beer commercial?"

"Come on, I'll show you."

Leading them to the falls and leaving them to wash up, she decided to do a little exploring up the ravine. She climbed past the waterfall and picked her way carefully along to where the tiny creek frolicked out of high clay bluffs.

When the ravine became too narrow to negotiate easily, she pulled herself onto the bank and found herself in upland forest, pine needles underfoot. As she padded along, sidestepping saw-briars, she noticed blue overhead. The clouds were blowing away, leaving the afternoon clean and crisp.

If only she could keep ascending, she felt certain she would find a road. For some reason, she thought about Bartram Oliver and that concert she had missed. Then she glanced down and halted suddenly.

Two copperheads lay, one in front of the other, just two feet away, motionless, heads up. Another move and she would have stepped on them with her bare feet. One slid its tongue out to test the air.

She took a cautious step back. At a safe distance, she eyed them curiously. She thought snakes were solitary creatures, yet here were two together. Perhaps they were preparing to mate. She pondered with a shiver how close she had come to their fangs.

She heard the two men come up behind her. "Wait," she whispered. "Snakes."

Calvin edged alongside and saw them. Cursing, he grabbed a stick and struck furiously at them. He hit one in the body and it writhed broken-backed while its companion coiled up, head back, ready to strike.

"Calvin, what are you doing?" Cindy said. "They weren't hurting anything."

Ignoring her, he bludgeoned the second one. The snakes twisted around each other in a dying tangle, and he hit them repeatedly until she grabbed his arm in dismay. He swung around, and she saw the old violence in his eyes.

He threw the stick down angrily. "Let's go!" he said, and plunged ahead.

Shaken, Cindy took Nick's hand. "Come on, Grandpa."

CHAPTER 21

At sunset Cindy spotted an opening in the forest up ahead. Leaving her grandfather with Calvin, she dashed forward, expecting to find a field, pasture, or road. Instead she came out onto a high bluff overlooking the river.

When the two men joined her, she had dropped to her knees, sobbing silently. Seeing the wide brown water below them, Calvin cursed and began kicking the leaves underfoot. He turned his anger on her.

"You stupid woman. You took us in a circle! Look what you did!"

She hung her head as if truly guilty.

Nick stepped past both of them to the very lip of the bluff. He inhaled deeply. "That's it," he said dreamily. "The river. I knew we'd be back."

"You're crazy, old man," Calvin said.

Nick turned toward him, beaming. "You don't understand, nephew. You got to open yourself to the will of the Lord."

"I'm fed up with the will of the Lord," Calvin retorted. "I been all day with the will of the Lord, and all it's got me is worser off." Then he cupped his hands to his mouth and bellowed obscenities at the river, the forest, the world at large.

"That's enough, Calvin," Cindy said suddenly, rising to her feet. "We're not going to go through all that again."

He spun around and grabbed her shoulders roughly. "That right, cousin?"

She rammed her knee into his groin, doubling him over. As he dropped to his knees, she picked up a stick and raised it over her head.

"That's right!" she said. "You've got no gun, you've got no knife, and if you try any more of your tricks, you'll forevermore regret it. Hear me?"

"Why'd you have to go and do that?" he moaned.

Nick placed his hand on Calvin's head and began to murmur a prayer. Calvin shook the hand off. "I don't want your prayers, old man. You'll get yours. You too, cousin."

"Can't we stop this?" she shouted. "We're all in this together. If we stick together, we'll get out. Whatever your problems are, at least put them on hold till we get out of here. All right?"

He got shakily to his feet. "All right, all right. Only, what I want to know is, what do we do now?"

She peered down the river. "Look," she said, pointing. "Is that a camphouse?"

He squinted with his one good eye. "Sho 'nuff is, sweetheart. Now you're using your head."

"It's going to be rough," she warned. "It must be seventy feet straight down, and the sun's almost gone. And even when we do get down, it must be half a mile to the camp."

"It can't be no worse than what we've been through already, can it?" Calvin said with a grin.

"I guess not. Come on, Grandpa. It's a long way down."

———

Unable to find an easy descent, they decided to go straight down the side of the bluff. Slipping and sliding on the steep clay bank, grabbing vines and roots and crumbling clay, they reached a narrow shelf several feet above water level. Picking their way along it, they entered the dark forest, which hummed with creatures heralding the approaching night.

"We might as well stop here," Cindy said. "I can't see where I'm putting my feet."

"I'd a heap rather reach that camp," Calvin said.

"We just can't do it. The bugs aren't too bad here. Let's just wait for daylight."

They sat down and tried to get comfortable.

"Reckon we ought to build a fire?" asked Calvin.

"With what?"

"Listen! What's that?" A deep, rumbling sound came from the nearby river.

"I don't know."

"Listen. Hear it?"

"Bullfrogs?" Cindy guessed.

Nick laughed. "That's a gator," he said. "Big bull gator. This is his home we're in, chirrun."

Cindy scooted closer to him. "Not really—is it?"

Nick chuckled gently. "You'll be all right, sugar."

"What's he mean, 'all right'?" Calvin said. Cindy could hear fear in his voice.

"I guess he means the bull gator always goes for a man first," she teased. "They get the young men first and leave the women for last."

"You lying."

She giggled mischievously. "The big bull gator sneaks through the woods at night looking for something to eat—something just about your size, Calvin."

He laughed nervously. "You're cute, sister, you really are. Now stow that jive."

"Isn't that right, Grandpa?" Cindy asked innocently. "The gator goes for the man first?"

"'And the fear of you shall be upon every beast upon the earth,'" Nick quoted. "That's in Genesis."

"What's he saying?" Calvin asked. "Old man, are you talking that crazy Bible talk again?"

"The Lord Jesus got you in his power, only you don't know it yet," Nick replied. "You'll find out in due time."

Calvin snorted. "Jesus. Alligators. Quit talking all this scary talk. Let's get some sleep."

"Sleep then, Calvin. Who's stopping you?" Cindy taunted, unable to stifle the satisfaction she felt at seeing him frightened. "You're not afraid of the dark, are you?"

"Listen! There it is again!"

The deep-throated bellow seemed to shake the ground, putting a chill on Cindy's sarcasm. "Are you sure it's all right, Grandpa?"

He patted her arm. "Sleep, child," he whispered.

Calvin swatted his face. "Mosquitoes! I thought you said there weren't no bugs."

Cindy sighed and curled up next to her grandfather, closing her eyes.

"I think we ought to go on and try to find that camp now," Calvin persisted.

"Go ahead," Cindy murmured. "We'll see you in the morning."

But he didn't stir, except to bat at mosquitoes and wriggle down into the damp leaves.

━━━━━━━━━

A full moon silvered the forest. In its pale glow Cindy saw her grandfather and Calvin both asleep. She rose and padded on bare feet to the river, flowing in grandeur, silent under the moonlight.

Strangely, she felt no fear of the river or gators or snakes. Through the tree limbs, stars glimmered in the moon-milky sky. The air was cool and clammy. She fancied she smelled the Gulf of Mexico, but of course it must be too far off.

Her problems, too, seemed distant. She was alone in the hollow hand of night, treading in a pool of lunar light, dancing the river dance. She had waltzed with copperheads and bathed under waterfalls. She had waded to her armpits like Katharine Hepburn in *The African Queen*. She had fought a man—a violent man—and won. She had guided them through the swamp—not to safe haven, perhaps, but at least back to the river. A camp was nearby, and they would flag the next fisherman.

Her grandfather's eyelids had begun to ooze pus; an odor came from his face that scared her. Calvin also was bad off. She needed to get them both to a doctor soon. The swamp air was no balm to their wounds.

And hungry? She was famished. She had drunk frequently from the streams, with no apparent damage to her insides, but she'd been a day without sufficient food, engaged in hard exercise. Maybe they could find a way into the camphouse and locate something to eat.

The river looked so gentle just now, a wide road. She wished she could walk onto it, as she used to ice skate up north.

From the camp she would get someone to fetch a rescue boat from Three Rivers Landing. And after Calvin was patched up—well, he would have to go on and face the justice he deserved for threatening their lives.

She had survived Calvin *and* the swamp. Help was near.

In the past days her passions had careened wildly, from grief to anger to terror to peace—and now utter fatigue. She stretched out on her side in full view of the dreamy river and danced into slumber.

———

A beaver climbed out of the river and perched on a log in the rosy dawn light. From her prone position on the ground, Cindy watched as the large, furry rodent nibbled the bark off a stick it held in its front paws. What a handsome animal! Fine, noble, dignified—at home here. It blinked, oblivious to the beauties of nature around it: the colorful dawn breaking on reefs of pure blue, backed by silver whitecaps of cloud. As the beaver nibbled, Cindy could almost taste the pungent, sap-flavored wood, grainy and coarse.

Suddenly the creature froze. A look of alarm came into its eyes. Something awful was coming; some evil presence lurked nearby.

The beaver was in the act of turning when a huge alligator exploded from beneath the surface of the water, clamping its huge jaws down onto the head of its prey. The victim's squeals broke the stillness of the dawn, its screams of terror surprisingly human-like. Shaking its long scaly body—twice as long as a man—the gator backed down into the water, pulling the thrashing beaver with it. Both disappeared under the surface, and it was as if they never existed. The stick the beaver had been eating, caught in the current, swirled downstream.

Cindy sat up gasping.

It was still night. There was no log, no dawn, no carnage.

She pulled herself to the river and splashed cold water onto her face. Remembering the monster of her dream, she recoiled, scrambling back to where the two men lay sleeping.

Shaking, inwardly sobbing with fear, she curled up next to her grandfather and held onto his damp, tattered denim coat.

Please, God, she prayed, *get us out of here soon.*

CHAPTER 22

A plank of indeterminate soundness led from the bank to the floating camphouse. It had taken them hours to traverse the half-mile or so of riverside jungle—an ordeal of vines, briars, mud, and insects.

Cindy tested the plank and found it springy but firm. She gingerly led Nick across, coaxing him gently. On board the narrow, covered deck she rapped on the door to the cabin. No one answered. She tried the doorknob. Locked.

Around the corner, Calvin peered in the windows. "I see cabinets. Hey, there's a loaf of bread. And some ketchup. I could eat bread and ketchup right now, I sure could."

Cindy flinched when she heard the sound of shattering glass. "Calvin! What are you doing?"

"Chow time, sister."

She heard him open the window and climb in. When he didn't unlock the door, she banged on it. "Come on, let us in!"

Calvin opened the door, his mouth full of bread. An open loaf, moldy around the edges, lay on the table. Cindy and Nick entered the musty room, and

Calvin began ransacking cupboards, pulling down cans of sardines, a jar of peanut butter, and plastic soda bottles full of water. Soon they were feasting on the spoils, guzzling tepid water between mouthfuls.

"I've never been so hungry in my life," Cindy said.

Calvin laughed. "It's good, ain't it? Get hungry enough and you'll do anything. Ain't that right, Unk?"

Eating sparingly from a piece of bread smeared with peanut butter, the old man grinned and smacked his lips. His awkward attempts to eat without seeing left his face dotted with peanut butter.

When Cindy finished eating, she got up to look around. "I wonder if this stove works," she mused, twisting a knob without effect.

"Put a match to it," Calvin said, pointing to the box of matches on the shelf above the stove.

When she did, the gas burner flared to life.

"All right!" Cindy said. "Now let me see if I can find us some coffee. Anybody want coffee?"

"That'd be mighty nice," Nick said.

Calvin began searching the cabinets again. "Seems like at least they'd have a little liquor around here."

"I wish you'd stay away from that stuff, at least while we're out here," said Cindy.

He ignored her. "Aha! Here's something." He drew out a pint bottle containing a small amount of whiskey. "Better than nothing, I guess. Bottoms up!" He swigged it down and smacked his lips.

Cindy frowned at him. "Why don't you do something useful? See if you can find a first-aid kit or something?" she said. "That way I can patch you and Grandpa up."

"Good liquor's the only medicine I need," he sneered, and walked outside.

Cindy finished making coffee. "Here," she said, placing a steaming cup in front of her grandfather. "You drink it black, don't you?"

"Black, that's how I like it," he said, inhaling the aroma.

Cindy sipped hers as she looked around for a first-aid kit. She found one on the top shelf of a cabinet.

"Grandpa," she said softly, sitting down at the table across from him, "I've got some medicine here. Why don't you let me change that dressing? It's looking pretty awful."

A frown of concern crossed his face. "It's go'n hurt powerful, I know—but I 'spect we better," he agreed.

"Here, take these aspirin," she said, pressing three into his hand. "They'll help."

When he had swallowed them, she pulled her chair alongside his and went to work. The rag over his eyes was stuck in place by dried blood. As she moistened it and peeled it away, Nick groaned softly.

"It'll be over in a minute," she said.

Blackened blood clotted the wound, and he gripped the table edge, gritting his teeth, sweat pouring down his face, as she cleansed it. She squeezed ointment onto a folded strip of gauze and wrapped it into place.

"There," she said at last. "Why don't you go lie down awhile? I think I saw a bed in the back."

144

He nodded dully, and she led him into the single, cramped bedroom. She helped him down onto the bed, covering him with a faded quilt folded at the foot of the bare mattress.

"I'll be back to check on you in a little while," she said tenderly.

She left the room, closing the door, and went outside. Around back at a covered boat dock she found Calvin kneeling in a large flatbottom boat, tinkering with the motor. He looked up.

"We hit a gold mine, sister." He grinned. "These fools done left us a boat and motor. It's not even locked. When I get this baby fueled up, we'll be on our way."

Her instincts sounded a warning. "Uh, I don't think that's such a good idea."

"Huh?"

"Why don't we just wait here for help? Some fishermen will come by soon, I'm sure."

He stared at her. "Are you crazy? Just sit on this tub? We got a boat and a motor right here. We can hop in and go wherever we want."

"You go ahead," she said, edging back, suddenly afraid of him again. "Grandpa and I will stay here."

Calvin sprang toward her and she turned, racing along the narrow deck. As she reached the door of the cabin, Calvin grabbed the collar of her blouse. She tore free and lunged for a drawer where she had seen a butcher knife. He pounced on her, spinning her around and pinning her hands to the countertop.

"Oh no you don't, sister," he said, panting. He glanced around. "Where's the old man?"

"Sleeping."

He raised his hands to her shoulders. "Don't you think it's about time you and me had a little fun?" He dropped his hand quickly to block her rising knee. "That trick don't work twice, sweetie," he said. He grabbed her shoulders again and threw her roughly across the room.

Cindy looked around for a weapon, but he was on her again, shoving her against the wall, his monstrous face inches from hers. She writhed and tried to bite, but he easily overpowered her.

The bedroom door opened, and Nick stumbled out. He raised a hand and pointed in Calvin's direction. "Get thee behind me, Satan!"

Calvin picked up a water bottle and flung it at the old man. It struck his chest, knocking him back. Cindy broke free and ran for the door, but Calvin caught her and pulled her inside.

"Now, now," he taunted. "Don't fight it."

Some raw, new anger welled up inside her. Trapped in the room with this human predator, her grandfather's life as well as her own in danger, Cindy turned from fearful victim to angry contender.

Grabbing whatever came to hand—dish rack, plate, ketchup bottle—she began to hurl things at Calvin. He ducked, dodging everything except the coffeepot, which spilled steaming grounds across his face. As he fell to his knees, trying to wipe them away, she hoisted a chair and slammed it down onto his head. She kept hitting him until he slumped forward and lay still.

Heaving for breath, she stumbled outside and vomited into the river. She sank to her knees, trying to regain her strength, to dispel the awful, sickening violence that possessed her.

She heard a low voice and, afraid Calvin had recovered, rushed back inside. Her grandfather was kneeling beside the prostrate man, murmuring, "Lead us not into temptation, but deliver us from evil, for thine is the kingdom, the power and the glory forever, amen."

Cindy wept.

CHAPTER 23

The river air felt refreshing as they motored down the wide waterway with Cindy at the throttle, Nick in the bow, and Calvin hunched disconsolately amidships, his hands tied tightly behind his back with thick rope. Cindy congratulated herself silently. They should be at Three Rivers Landing soon, where they would hand Calvin over to the law and get medical help for her grandfather.

While Calvin lay unconscious back in the cabin, she had found some rope and tied his hands. Realizing it was senseless to wait indefinitely at the camp, she had then loaded the two men into the boat and cranked the motor. Nick told her how to operate the outboard, and after a little experimentation they were making tracks downriver.

The boat moved at astonishing speed, rounding one bend after another. They should be there any minute, Cindy thought. They had the upper hand now, the swamp itself subjugated to the power of their technology. She could go anywhere she wanted, and quickly. She felt exhilarated.

148

Calvin shook his head, slowly recovering his senses, looking around glumly.

Cindy told herself she would never trust him again, nor let him out of her power until the law took him. She could believe nothing he said. He was a sociopath through and through. At her side lay a butcher knife and a length of iron pipe, in the unlikely event he should give her problems.

But where was Three Rivers Landing?

Bend after bend passed, camp after empty camp. The river seemed deserted. Forest loomed on either side; the air stank sweetly of swamp. Sandbars were nowhere to be seen, and the weeds that grew at the edge had a sinister, marshy look.

Abruptly, the river ahead of them seemed to end—actually to come to a dead halt against a wall of forest. Cindy throttled down, looking about with a frown.

The Pascagoula split in a perfect T. One channel went right, the other left.

"Grandpa, we're at a fork," she said.

He sniffed the air.

"I don't know what happened to Three Rivers Landing," she said. "I don't understand it. We should have been there a long time ago. You suppose it's still there?"

"We must have passed it when we was in the swamp," Nick said.

Of course. They had made a big loop, no doubt bypassing the landing altogether. "Should we turn around and go look for it?"

Nick shook his head. "It can't be far to Pascagoula—the city. That's on the coast," he said. "We just follow this river and we'll get there."

"But which channel?"

"I seem to 'member hearing there was two rivers, a east one and a west one. They come together down at Pascagoula. So I guess it don't really matter."

Cindy turned the boat right, accelerating. After they rounded the first bend, the channel narrowed considerably. She eased back on the throttle, fearing hidden snags, and they rode slowly in the gloomy shade of afternoon shadows.

"This is eerie," she said to herself.

Nick continued to sniff the air like a hound, substituting smell for sight. "This is the Lord's country," he said.

"More like the devil's," Cindy mumbled.

The forest crowded right down to the banks, which rose only inches above the level of the river. She half expected to hear monkeys and parrots.

"There's something up ahead!" she said. It was a landing, surrounded by a cluster of camps. "It's a boat ramp, Grandpa. I don't think this is Three Rivers Landing, but whatever it is, we're going to get out of here now," she said.

She steered the boat up to the concrete ramp and killed the engine.

"Hello!" she called. "Anybody here?"

The answering silence was ominous. Tall trees towered around, surging with cricket moans.

"You two wait here," she said. Then, remembering Calvin's feet were free, she lashed them together. "I'm sorry, Calvin, but I can't afford to leave you untied."

150

He glared at her and grunted.

She climbed out of the boat and went to each of the camps and knocked, but there was no one around. Cobwebs and dirt gave the places a derelict appearance. At last she set off down the dirt road that led away from the landing, hoping at least to find a paved road or a country store.

Half a mile later, nothing had changed. No people, no parked vehicles, no sounds of distant traffic. Just a lonely, rutted track of cracked dirt overgrown with weeds, hemmed in by forest.

A hawk flew across the road in front of her, startling her.

"Creepy," she said aloud. "There's got to be somebody around here."

"I'm here, missy."

She spun around to see a grizzled white man holding a rifle. No taller than she, he wore tattered denim clothes stained with what appeared to be grease and blood and speckled with fish scales. Rubber boots came to his thighs. An absurdly battered felt hat perched on his head.

"Oh!" she said, then laughed. "You scared me."

The bluntness of his gaze cut her laughter short. Even from several yards away she smelled him, a mixture of fish, mud, and fermented sweat.

"Do you live here?" she asked.

Suddenly he swiveled, peering into the treetops. He raised the rifle, aimed, and fired. A flock of big black birds took wing from a dead cypress tree.

"Dang buzzards," he said, his scowl indicating he had missed.

She wanted to take flight too. The man's eyes

seemed deranged, and his strange stare did not inspire confidence.

"You ain't a reg'lar, are you?" the man said.

"Er—I'm sorry?" She chuckled nervously. "I don't catch your meaning, sir."

"A reg'lar! Them ain't one of your camps down to the river, is 'em?"

"N–no sir."

He nodded as if he had elicited some dark truth. "So who are you, then—and what you doing out in these woods?" He circled her as if searching for traces of criminality.

"My name's Cindy, Cindy Sharp," she said. "We were out on the river and my grandfather's gun went off and he's hurt bad. I mean it exploded on him—"

"Gun! What's he doing with a gun out here? It ain't hunting season!"

She wanted to ask him the same but didn't dare. "I don't know—for snakes, I guess." She saw no purpose in trying to explain about Calvin.

The man squinted again. "You ain't the one's been messing my yoyos, is you?"

"Your what?"

"Yoyos. Yoyos! Somebody's been stealing my crappie."

"Your what, sir?"

"Crappie. White perch! Sac-a-lait! Where was you raised?"

"Sir, we haven't touched your yoyos."

"'Bout my minner traps, then? Foolin' with them, are ye?"

"No sir, I haven't touched anything."

He stopped in front of her. "You fishing?"

"Well, yes, we were."

"How bad's your granddad hurt?"

"Pretty bad. His eyes—"

"Come on." He turned and set off into the forest. Cindy didn't move. He stopped and peered at her through the bushes. "Ain't you coming?"

"Where? I mean—"

He snorted. "To my house. Come on, dang ye!"

Startled by the outburst, she scampered after him. He led her into the forest, though she saw no path at all.

CHAPTER 24

The man did not slow his pace when they reached a broad expanse of flooded forest, plunging right on into the stagnant water. Cindy halted. This did not seem right, not at all.

The man stopped, perplexed. "What you waitin' fer?" He gesticulated with the gun, and she could not tell whether he meant to threaten or encourage. Unwilling to take any more chances, she waded tentatively out into the mire she had fought so hard to escape.

"Where are we going?" she said, hurrying to catch up.

He just grunted.

Her jeans, which had finally dried out, were wet again to the knees. The squishy mud underfoot and the cold water on her legs filled her with revulsion, prompting memories of her recent ordeals. Only now her dread of the swamp was compounded by fear of this strange, diminutive man whose funky hat bobbed up and down with each step he took. She entertained ideas of escaping—hiding behind a tree, or making a run for it—but he seemed too sharp for that. Besides, he was armed.

Cypress trees rose from the water around her. Golden sunlight fell through their greening branches, which were matted in places with Spanish moss. Up ahead a great blue heron took flight, gliding over the water on broad wings and arching up through the treetops out of sight. The man paid it no mind.

She heard a flurry of high-pitched, guttural cries and noticed a group of large, dark shapes milling about on a small piece of cane-choked high ground. At first the weird notion struck her that they had chanced upon a colony of Little People—leprechauns or swamp elves. The image did not seem at all incongruous in these bizarre surroundings.

The man stopped, raised a hand to his mouth, and imitated the noises. Cindy recognized the sound as a turkey yelp. Some of the shadow-dark forms stopped at the man's voice, but others, wiser, clucked and took flight in a crash of wings. The man raised his gun and aimed at the two or three that remained standing, bobbing their heads up and down in attempts to get a good look at the intruders. Cindy expected the crack of a gunshot, but the man just sighted down his barrel until the last birds flew away.

Lowering his rifle, he glanced back at her with a rotten-toothed grin. "Purty, ain't they?"

She nodded. "Why didn't you shoot?" she ventured.

He snorted. "I can get me a turkey any day of the

week when I get a hankering. Right now I got plenty t' eat." He resumed wading and she followed.

"This ain't always underwater," he said over his shoulder. "It'll start falling before long. Crawfishin's about to get right! When the water gets out of here it'll be dry near-about till Christmas, 'cept for sloughs and baygalls."

The swamp became shallower, giving way to thickets of marsh grass and arrowhead plants. Suddenly a house rose in front of them on stilts above the water—the most ramshackle dwelling she had ever seen, making the river camps look like palaces.

The man mounted rickety wooden steps, his boots leaving muddy pools, while Cindy stood below examining the area in wonder. Dozens of rusty steel traps hung by their chains from support posts. A variety of old tools crowded a table whose top was only a few feet above the water level. Stuck in every other dry spot was some sort of bucket, fish trap, wire, cable, chain, line, or hook.

"Well?" The man stood impatiently on the steps. "What you waiting for, anyhow?"

She could not bring herself to climb the steps—to enter that shack with this man.

"I–I'll just wait here in the—the yard," she said haltingly.

He smacked his lips in disbelief and came back down the steps. "I thought your grandpa was hurt."

"He is."

"Well, come on, then." He turned to go up again.

An inkling of instinct told her it would be all right to follow, but her entire intellect protested. Entering a swampbilly's shack with a gun-toting, seemingly demented backwoodsman didn't sound like the smartest thing she'd ever done. In the past days, however, she had learned to trust her instinct more than ever before in her life, so she followed him.

Opening the door, he led her through a tiny, roach-infested kitchen full of food-caked dishes to what was apparently the only other room, a small, dark place crammed with furniture. Except for the bed, everything was heaped with clothes, yellowed newspapers, books, and boxes.

The man began rummaging in a corner. "Gun blew up on him, huh?"

"Yessir." She examined the dungeon. Where did he go to the bathroom?

"Mud in the barrel?"

"Huh? Er, yessir. Sand."

He nodded, throwing clothes out behind him like a dog rooting through trash. "I had a friend that happened to onct. Korea. Ah." He pulled out a green metal box with a faded red cross on it.

Cindy noticed a framed black and white photo of soldiers, all young men, at the head of the dust-covered bedstead.

"Are you in here?" she asked, moving up for a closer look.

He nodded. "Front row, far right. Recognize me?"

She saw no resemblance. Beside that photo was a tinted portrait shot of a plump young woman, smiling, her chin resting on her hands. "And the woman?" Cindy asked.

"Bessie." Staring at the photo, he seemed lost in reverie. Cindy imagined she could hear his sad memories behind the curtain of a bereft present. A chill passed through her.

"I'm sorry," she said softly.

The man peered at her for a moment, then reached under a pillow and withdrew half a plug of tobacco.

"Ah! Here it is. I been starving for a chew." He put the square to his mouth and bit off a hunk. "C'mon."

He left the room, Cindy right behind him.

"We'll take my pirogue," he said when they reached the water, but she saw no boat as they waded into the swamp, following a slough that snaked into a thicket. Apparently a maze of such waterways crisscrossed this forest, joining one shallow lake to another.

"You can foller the bank if you can whack your way through them weeds," the man told her as the water deepened. "It gets deep up here sure 'nuff."

Without warning he dropped under, just managing to hoist the rifle and green box over his head in time to keep them dry. He came up sputtering.

"Dang! I miss that drop-off ever' time." Grinning, he spat a stream of brown juice into the almost-as-brown water. "Watch fer it now."

She glided out, swimming over the deep hole till she found bottom again.

"The pirogue's right up here," the man said, poking through the bushes.

Suddenly he jumped back, almost losing his footing, as the area in front of him exploded with mud and water-spray.

"Look out!" he yelled, struggling to raise his gun.

Cindy watched in amazement as a huge alligator lunged, writhed, and hit the water like heavy artillery, disappearing under it, moving away from them. The man fired belatedly, the bullet pinging as it echoed off the surface.

"Son of a gun nestin' under my pirogue!" he declared indignantly, flipping the boat over to reveal a sizable wallow. "Good thing she didn't have no young 'uns yet or you'd a done seen a ruckus! Come on, give me a hand washing these spiders out."

With unsteady hands she helped him slosh water into the mud-caked boat.

"Will it be safe to go down here now, with that gator?" she asked.

"Safe? Safe!" He threw his head back and laughed. "By garly, by garly." He craned over, staring her in the eye, tobacco juice leaking down his chin. "By garly, miss, there ain't nothin' safe. Nothin'! Don't you know that?"

His statement struck her like a revelation. This whole malevolent swamp had encased her in a tangled, inescapable grip. She trembled as fear spun fast silver webs through her body.

Then, almost as quickly, she relaxed. The man, laughing and choking on his tobacco juice, was right. If nothing, ever, was safe, then what was the point of fear? She found herself laughing with him. Pleased that she shared his joke, he swatted his boots with his hat, revealing a pale, nearly bald head that looked far older than the rest of him.

"That's good," he said, nodding vigorously. Standing awkwardly in shallow water, he poured several gallons of water out of his hip boots, then searched in the bushes for a pole and paddles.

159

"Get in and let's go," he told her. "It'll be dark in a few hours."

Cindy climbed gingerly into the front of the tiny, canoe-like craft with its flat bottom and flared hull. Her every move rocked the boat, which felt as if it would flip at any moment, but the man stepped carelessly in and shoved off with the pole. The pirogue glided like a water spider down the channel.

"Yes, yes!" he shouted, spitting as far as he could. "You in my country now. You in Tom Hunt's country. Yes you is." He frowned. "What'd you say your name was?"

"Cindy," she said hastily.

He beamed, revealing awful teeth. "That's right. Cindy. To the rescue, Cindy."

———————

The slough became a sluggish creek wending between low, muddy banks. Because of low-hanging branches and over-arching logs, Tom Hunt sat down in the back of the boat, substituting a paddle for his pole. Cindy used the other paddle, ducking her head often to avoid dangling limbs, always watching for snakes.

The creek made a hard bend and she saw the river before them, wide and bright under the blue sky.

"I didn't even notice this creek when we passed by," she said.

"You'll miss plenty a thang in the swamp if yer not watching," Tom Hunt said.

As he swung the boat onto the main river, she shipped her paddle. "Mr. Hunt, there's something I need to tell you before we get there."

He looked at her questioningly.

"My grandpa's not the only one I'm with," she said. "You see, my cousin—well, he tried to kidnap us and I had to tie him up."

"Tie 'm up?" Hunt raised his eyebrows.

"Yessir. See, it's because of him that my grandpa got shot."

"I thought you said he had sand in the barrel."

"But it was my cousin Calvin who held the gun on us in the first place. Grandpa took it away, and somehow the barrel got clogged and—"

Hunt nodded thoughtfully. "So what we got here's a dangerous situation. Good thing I'm per-pared." He patted the rifle beside him in the boat.

"He's tied up now. I think it will be all right," Cindy said, resuming her paddling. "But I am worried about my grandpa. It's been two days now. He needs to see a doctor bad."

"We'll take care of 'm. Don't you worry none."

They drifted in the shadows close to the bank, the forest looming alongside. Rounding a bend, Cindy spotted the ramp and the boat up ahead.

"That's it," she said, pointing.

Before the words were fully out of her mouth, the pirogue erupted into the air and she found herself spilled into the cold, muddy river. She came up gasping, picturing the giant alligator exacting re-venge.

But when her eyes cleared, she saw two men thrashing in chest-deep water. Calvin had hold of the rifle and was striking Tom Hunt in the head. Hunt crumpled, and Calvin grabbed him by his collar, pulling him onto the muddy shore. Then he stood up and leveled the gun at Cindy.

"Get over here—now!" He was dripping wet and savagely angry.

Hunt moaned and Calvin wheeled around, gunstock poised to strike. When he saw the man was barely conscious, he stepped close to him, paused, then leaned over and, pinching Hunt's cheeks, forced his mouth open. With his right hand he inserted the narrow barrel of the .22 into the woodsman's mouth.

"Calvin, no!" Cindy screamed, full of nightmare visions. She splashed out of the water.

He backhanded her without looking and flicked the safety off the gun.

"Calvin—think what you're doing!"

He stopped and straightened, the gun barrel lolling on Hunt's lips. Then he laughed. "You know, you're right, cousin. Last thing I need's another murder rap." He kicked the fallen man in the ribs, eliciting a groan, then leaned over to pull him into the weeds out of sight.

Finally he faced Cindy, who rested on her knees at the river's edge.

"Game's over, sister," he said. "Fetch me that boat and let me explain a few things to you."

He squatted on the bank while she splashed out and wrestled the overturned pirogue to shore. He made no offer to help as she struggled to turn over the water-heavy craft and empty it.

"All right, here's the plan," Calvin said after she had gathered up the floating wooden paddles and was kneeling, panting, beside the boat. "We ain't go'n have no more of your jive. You get smart with me one more time and, pftt, that's it, Uncle Nick is dead, no questions asked. Got me?"

She nodded.

"Now you're gonna row me down to that boat and we're gonna get out of this swamp. Got me?"

She nodded.

"Seems like I heard the old man say this river comes out to a town of some kind. We're go'n get there quicktime and dump that motorboat. Trade it in on a new car, you might say. What kind of car you like, sugar? Big limo, or jazzy sports car—like your little red one? Well, we'll just see what comes our way. But I ain't go'n have no more trouble out of you, understand?"

She nodded.

"Once we get to town, well then, we'll just have to see what happens. I still got my eye on Miami. The fast life. We may ditch the old man and you and me go cruising on the open highway. How's that sound?"

She didn't answer.

"How's that sound!"

"Fine."

He grinned. "Better. You learning. You just got to be tamed down is all. And I'm just the man for the job, cousin." He stood up and stretched. "I don't know where you got all that grit anyhow. Must run in the family. You're as mean as me, near-about. Know that, girl?"

She shrugged.

"One other thing—remind me to teach you how to

tie a decent knot sometime." He rubbed his wrists. "Now let's get a move on."

She waited meekly till he was in the pirogue, then climbed in, glancing sadly back to the bushes where Tom Hunt lay.

CHAPTER 25

Calvin drove the boat like a race car, careening around bends, careless of hidden dangers. The river widened quickly after the landing, forest giving way to marsh grass. Soon not a tree was in sight except for sparse clumps of willows or cypress, some of them dotted with flocks of white egrets. To the south, thunderheads rose in orange and white stacks, catching the lowering sunlight.

The west river merged with the east and they entered a broad expanse, the boat skipping *pap-pap-pap* over the water. Cindy sniffed deeply; the sea air was unmistakable now.

They passed a houseboat, then a shrimper, rounded a curve and saw the city of Pascagoula scattered along a coastal highway. To their left shipyards sprawled in a jumble of iron and rust. Calvin hugged the right bank, slowing as they approached the final bridge on the river. Through it they saw open water and felt the direct onslaught of Gulf breezes from the Mississippi Sound. On the left bank, just this side of the bridge, Cindy spotted a marina with a cove full of boat docks. Calvin throttled down and steered toward it.

As he turned into the cove, Cindy saw a police car and heard Calvin curse at the same time. Beside the car, parked with both doors open by the docks, two uniformed men stood peering across the water.

Calvin made a sharp U-turn, picking up speed, his furious curses forming a counterpoint to the motor's whine. Even taking into account his fear and anger, Cindy was not prepared when he turned south on the river, passing under the bridge and heading for the open sea.

"Calvin!" she said, pivoting. "What are you doing?"

He ignored her. Frowning in disbelief, she quickly snatched up the boat's two life vests.

"Here, put this on, Grandpa," she said to Nick, who had sat stoically in front ever since the incident at the landing. She helped him into the life vest, then slipped on the other, zipping it up tightly and buckling it around her waist.

"You're going to get us all killed!" she shouted above the roar of the wind and motor.

"Shut up and turn around!"

She obeyed angrily. On their right they passed low-lying clumps of marsh, the continent's dying gasps. In the metallic sunlight far ahead she saw whitecaps dancing in the gusty wind. Beyond them lay a tiny scrap of land topped by a finger of lighthouse. Calvin headed straight for it.

"Calvin," she pleaded, "it's miles to that island. Please turn around!"

He leaned forward and backfisted her, bloodying

her lip. Tears sprang to her eyes and she looked away.

As they left the last shelter of land, the boat began to toss about roughly, despite the powerful motor. The wind threw brine into their faces; breakers sloshed over the sides, drenching them. Calvin angled directly into the waves, hitting them head-on despite their ruthless battering.

Cindy took a deep breath of the crisp, damp, salty air. In the west the sun paved a staircase of clouds with ruddy gold. Seagulls nicked their wheeling silhouettes against the sky. To the east she noticed what appeared to be a high concrete seawall close by. It made no sense for such a structure to be built so far out. The next moment she recognized it as a rogue wave probably ten feet high.

"Look!" she shouted.

Calvin saw it at the same time, moving ineluctably toward them off the lee bow.

"Hold on, Grandpa!" Cindy shouted, reaching for the old man.

Calvin yanked the tiller for a starboard turn, but the wave beat him to the draw.

The underside of the Mississippi Sound was amber-green and silent, Cindy discovered.

Then she was up, gasping, in time to hear the tinny whine of the upside-down motor choke into silence. Seawater filled her belly, nose, and mouth. She coughed violently, thrashing about—and thought immediately of sharks.

The Hattiesburg newspaper occasionally showed

photos of Gulf fishermen hoisting big bulls, makos, even hammerheads caught in these waters. She slowed the frantic kicking of her legs and looked around.

"Grandpa!" she shouted.

He was bobbing a short distance away, held afloat by his vest. He waved when he heard her cry. Then she heard Calvin.

"Help! Help me! I can't swim!"

Cindy spun around in the water. Calvin was perched precariously atop the overturned boat, wallowing and pitching in the choppy seas. Just then a large wave knocked him off and he came up snorting, struggling in panic to get back on.

"Help me! Help me!" he shouted in a gargled, fear-pitched voice.

While she debated what to do, Cindy noticed her grandfather swimming toward Calvin. To her astonishment she saw that he had removed his life vest and was holding it high in one hand.

"Calvin!" he shouted. "Where are you?"

"Help me, Uncle Nick!"

Gauging Calvin's position by his voice, Nick yelled "Catch!" and threw the vest. Calvin lunged for it, falling off the boat again. This time it flipped. While he wrestled with the vest, the boat filled and sank.

A wave smashed Cindy's face. She turned her back to the wind-driven water to clear her nose and eyes. When she looked back around, she saw Calvin floating several yards away gripping the life vest.

Her grandfather was nowhere in sight.

CHAPTER 26

"Grandpa!" Cindy paddled about like a confused, frightened puppy. "Grandpa!"

"Cindy!"

She spun quickly, only to see Calvin bouncing up and down in the waves.

"Where's Grandpa?" she called.

He shook his head, rubbing his eyes. "Swim for the island!" he shouted, pointing. "We can make it!" He sounded more afraid to be left alone than concerned for her safety.

She turned away, disgusted at his selfish lack of concern for the old man. She lunged up for a better view, but saw only an angry terrain of dark blue. In the west the sun was going down in golden splendor as if this were just another day.

Several such leaps left her exhausted and disoriented. She swiveled in the water just in time to catch a faceful of brine. Gasping and blowing, she turned her back to the force.

When she quit treading, she had the sensation she was sinking, and for a panicked moment thought her life vest did not work. But an instant later it buoyed her up safely.

She thought back over every detail of the disaster. From the landing on, everything had gone wrong. For that matter, the entire trip had been a fiasco. What made Calvin head out to sea like that? What a stupid stunt!

And thinking of that instant when the wave hit, she experienced again that surge of panic just before it struck. Yet there had been no interim, no sensation of actually falling. One minute in the boat, the next minute underwater in that green, bubbly silence.

She shivered.

Was her grandfather strong enough to stay afloat? And what about all those heavy clothes? And even if he could, where could he swim to, blind? A chilling image of him sinking, mouth agape in the amber-green, passed through her like an electric jolt. She saw a shark weaving tensely after his descending body, taking it like a fishing lure. . . .

No!

She retched into the water. Heaving and choking, she suddenly understood that she could do nothing for her grandfather or anyone else. Right now it was her own survival that was at stake.

Dizzy, nauseous, and confused, she tried to regain her equilibrium as she tossed up and down, water pouring relentlessly over her back and head. Her mouth fouled by bile and brine, she longed for just a taste of fresh water.

Where was the island anyway? Her salt-blurred eyes could distinguish nothing. She remembered that the wind had been coming out of the southeast.

If she swam with her back to it, maybe she could reach the mainland, depending on the tide.

She swam a stroke and doubled over immediately with nausea. She had not realized how sick she was—her body rebelling against all the seawater she'd swallowed and this constant buffeting.

Master yourself and swim, she commanded. She tried again and got the dry heaves.

When she recovered, she decided just to let the life vest carry her. *The trick is to conserve energy,* she told herself. This was going to be a waiting game—wait for the seas to calm, the nausea to pass, a boat to appear, or land to come into sight.

Or death to arrive.

No! No, she would fight it.

Her grandfather's voice rose gently in her mind: "I've got these blues, I'm not satisfied. . . ."

She had the blues now, yes she did.

━━━━━━━━

Sunset passed in a long blaze of vertigo and brine. Her body was chilled from the sea, and her dizziness was so intense she had to close her eyes. Best to keep sensation out. Just concentrate on breathing.

She wished she had a sip of fresh water, just to get the bad taste out of her mouth. The chop tossed her every which way, increasing her dizziness. She longed for smooth, regular swells. Unexpected waves kept popping up and flooding her mouth, nose, and ears.

After what seemed a long time she opened her eyes. Seeing a deep pink glow, she imagined for a moment she had died. The glow came from God and his court, over the horizon. When she felt better she would journey over there. Even from here she could feel an aura of peace and joy.

The image faded, and she recognized it as the afterglow of sunset.

"I hates to see that evening sun go down," she remembered her grandfather singing. But actually she felt a little better now. The waves weren't really that bad. She could handle them as long as she didn't swallow the saltwater. The vest would keep her afloat even if she were unconscious. She no longer kicked or struggled. There was no real reason for sharks to come—she hoped—unless they had already honed in on her earlier movements and were on the way.

Don't borrow trouble, she told herself. She remembered the story of Jesus calming the storm when the disciples were full of fear and doubt. *Peace, be still. God will get me out of this*, she thought.

But a chill passed over her at the notion that, if God had any hand in this at all, it was only to lead her inexorably to her doom.

The evening star appeared, and the ocean chop gradually evened out into more rhythmic swells. As the last light faded from the sky, Cindy kept her eyes open, hoping to see the lights of shore or a boat.

She had read somewhere that sharks were more active at night. If they came, she would not be able to see them, just hear the electric hiss of their fins. The idea made her insides sizzle; she became panicky, her heart pounding.

"Please, God," she prayed, looking up.

The sky was awash in stars. She had never seen so many, so brilliant. She leaned back and watched the pinpoints of light. In contrast with the turbulent, violent day, the night seemed soft and quiet, a pastoral symphony.

The ocean had become a range of hills. She rode to the top and slid down their backs—a long, smooth, lovely ride. With the wind and chop abated, she faced a rolling plain of reflected starlight, like riding a Ferris wheel at night—only this wheel rolled on forever, and she had a perpetual ticket.

Night lasts forever, she realized. It doesn't end when day comes. It keeps on anyway, unseen. Day is cosmetic, sunlight a thin lie. It's always night underneath. She wondered why she had never realized that simple fact before. Now she rode on the line of night, and though day might come eventually, she would still be on the night line. Daylight actually destroyed sight instead of granting it. Real vision came in the dark. That's when God would speak to her, finally, in whispers and sighs.

She could truly see for the first time in her life. She saw the rolling prairie of the seas, the numberless dimensions of the heavens.

She remembered her companions. Where was Calvin now? Her grandfather? The island? She saw only dark sea and sky.

If her grandfather was dead, he wasn't so bad off after all. He would be floating facedown on the same swells she rode, able to see now, his vision perfect. He could stare straight into the black and see it all. No more illusions for him.

The thought of her grandfather made her feel

warm and happy. In such a short time he had touched her life in a special way. She cried, and her tears tasted of ocean.

———————

Sometime in the night the cold began to crowd out her thoughts. Her hands reached to pull up her sleeping bag before she remembered where she was. She recalled reading that hypothermia, not drowning, was the real threat to a person adrift at sea.

She hugged herself to stay warm. The sea wrapped around her like a cold shawl. She closed her eyes and tried to envision a campfire. She could see the blaze; she put her hands out to it. If only she could keep it there by the force of her imagination.

Dozing off, she shivered and dreamed of glaciers. Canadian ice sheets slid south along the continent, leveling Philadelphia, crunching Mississippi's pine trees flat before pausing at the Gulf coast in blue-ice walls.

Cold water slapped her face, waking her. She tried to lick her lips; her thirst was becoming as bad as the cold. The inside of her mouth still tasted of salt, but the worst thing was the craving deep down in her body—not for something sweet like a soft drink but for fresh spring water flowing from the side of a hill. A waterfall bubbling down a mountainside, silver clear, sliding and frothing between lichened rocks crowded with fir trees and juniper bushes. Scented with evergreen, purified by moss, frigid from the mountain's heart. Gallons and gallons pouring down!

At this very instant untold millions of gallons of

drinking water rushed down mountainsides, ignored and wasted. Such a crime! She promised herself that if she survived she would never take fresh water for granted again.

She remembered in grammar school getting truly thirsty on the playground. She and her girlfriend had asked permission to go inside for a drink but the teacher refused, so they lay in the grass and fantasized about water. Their first idea was that teachers should install fountains at each student's desk. What if—what if trees were fountains? What if every blade of grass was a fountain? Everything on earth a water fountain?

Tormented from lack of sleep and physical misery, Cindy's thoughts ranged wild. Morality, civilization—all was a chimera dependent on the presence of drinking water, she concluded. Take that away and ethics would go out the window. What were living creatures anyway but receptacles for water? Fish, for instance, were simply swimming packets of sweet juices. Plants, animals, people—all living water jugs. The whole world functioned directly because of water. How could she not have realized that before? Evaporation, condensation, respiration, perspiration, urination, copulation—birth, death—all a transformation of water.

A wavelet sloshed against her face and she almost—almost—drank.

No! She must wake up. Had she been sleeping? She had to clear her head, forget her woes.

She wanted to drink the breeze, it felt so liquid. She tried to open her mouth, but her tongue clogged it. Some of the breeze slipped in and she swallowed, but it didn't help.

A numbness had moved out to her extremities. Fingers, toes, hands, feet, arms, legs—in a way, they were all superfluous, she reasoned. The main thing, after all, was this block of organs that kept her head working. Hands and feet were such useless items. They performed all sorts of meaningless tasks, getting her into trouble.

Now that she thought about it, it didn't matter much if a shark did come and tear off an arm or leg, as long as she didn't bleed too much. She had read that's what sharks did anyway, usually. They bit a leg or arm and spat it out and swam off. Apparently they didn't care much for human flesh.

I wonder what time it is. Surely dawn can't be far off. Where is that old knothead of a sun, anyway? She examined the black sky like a frozen explorer peering at the ashes of a dead campfire. *You old codger, you old rascal*, she said to the sun. *Get up, wake up. Get out here and go to work. Don't you know you've got a job to do?*

Nothing happened and, growing tired of waiting, she dozed off again.

A splash to her right awakened her. Looking around in the darkness, she thought she glimpsed the outline of a boat. *Grandpa!* It was Grandpa in his flatbottom boat—wasn't it? She couldn't quite make him out; he stayed just out of sight. But she thought she detected him with her peripheral vision.

Maybe it wasn't her grandfather. Maybe it was Calvin, hunting her down! Cindy spun in circles but couldn't sight him.

But no, this paddler had a friendly aura. Maybe it was a stranger, some tough but kindly guardian of the seas keeping an eye on her, making sure everything was all right. She appreciated that.

Despite the darkness, she spotted an island close by. It had picture-perfect palm trees, white beaches, and a crowd of strong-limbed young people in loincloths and grass skirts, smiling and waving, holding up green coconuts sloshing with cool juice. The straw huts behind them looked so cozy. Soon she would wash ashore and the islanders would hoist her with their strong brown arms and carry her into a hut. They would strip off these cold, wet, stiff clothes and pour warm coconut milk over her body to wash away the salt and soreness, then dry her thoroughly and lay her on a heap of blankets. By the light of a toasty campfire they would sing her to sleep with rich, deep-toned songs.

The island was gone now, but she knew it waited for her, just out of sight.

"Blues grabbed me at midnight, didn't turn me loose till day," her grandfather sang in her mind. "I didn't have nobody to drive these blues away."

She heard the dip of the boatman's paddle and felt grateful he was still there, even though her island wasn't.

Somehow it no longer mattered that she was cold. She understood that such sensations were illusory. Cold, heat, pleasure, pain—what a lot of nonsense! Sensations were mere luxuries anyway, like clothes to be taken off or put on at will. She had no use for them now. She was on the night line and had no use for folly or illusion.

She thought of God. She had never given him much attention, rather taking him for granted, not taking him seriously—too much nonsense associated with him. She had just pegged God as one more human folly, whether he existed or not. She only contemplated his existence now that all her other illusions were gone.

She realized she had been approaching him backward, so to speak—through the filter of her own follies.

She was rid of her follies now, every single one of them. She had nothing left but her core—even her arms and legs lacked feeling. Shed of every foible and illusion she had cloaked herself with throughout her life, she stared open-eyed into the black, cold infinity of the void. If God was anywhere, he would be here now.

A barely perceptible splash sounded to her right, and she remembered the boatman.

With a flood of illumination she realized that it wasn't her grandfather, Calvin, or any other person shadowing her in these dark wastes.

And she laughed out loud.

CHAPTER 27

The night became a circus: clowns bashing cymbals and squirting her with trick lapel flowers; swimming dogs yanking at her clothes; lunatics banging untuned guitars. Their crazy racket would not let her sleep.

With dawn the commotion faded, and she began to come to herself. All her insights and clear thinking had degenerated into confusion. Her vision was blurred. Her mouth felt like someone had stuffed a sock in it. Her ears and nose were full of mucus. Her limbs had no feeling. She drifted like kelp.

Gradually the sky brightened, and as her vision cleared she discovered with a jolt that the island—the real island—lay directly in front of her, a short distance away. Lowering her feet, she found that she could touch bottom.

Summoning all her power, she waded ashore. When she reached the sandy beach she stumbled and fell, but it did not matter anymore. She was on dry ground.

She fell into a hot, torturous, but somehow satisfying sleep in which her body seemed like a blisteringly heavy rucksack attached to her soul. She did not even come fully awake when strong arms hoisted her and dragged her into cool shade.

"Cindy. Cindy."

Calvin's voice did not surprise her. She just connected the dots of logic: he had swum to the island; she'd drifted. One way or the other, it had sucked them both in.

"Calvin." Her tongue fumbled stickily on her palate. "Water."

He disappeared. Looking up, she saw perfect blue sky past a rim of ragged green treetops. She floated off and then he was kneeling beside her, cupping a large, curved leaf to her sandpaper lips.

"It's swampish but sweet," he said.

She drank—most of it spilling down her chin— and he disappeared again. He returned with more, and she thought of a parent bird bringing bits of food, never enough, to famished chicks. The water both cooled and stung her mouth, but what mattered was what it did to her deep inside, spreading out in a healing glow.

Eventually her body reached a partial state of repair, and she slipped into a sweeter sleep than she had known before.

She dreamed she stood at the water closet on her grandfather's porch staring into the enamel pail full of pure, cool well water. She wanted to scoop up a dipperful and drink, but her arms were numb, unable to move. Though the day was hot, a cool breeze swept across the porch now and then. In the background, her grandfather played his guitar and sang softly:

180

"The big star fallin', mama 'tain't long for day,
The big star fallin', mama 'tain't long for day,
Maybe the sunshine will drive these blues away."

Something tickled her face; she snorted and shook her head. Opening her eyes, she saw Calvin sitting beside her, gently waving a leafy branch over her face.

"Horseflies," he explained.

She looked about, perplexed, then pulled herself up to a sitting position. Dizziness reigned in her skull.

"What happened?" she asked as he lay the branch aside. "Where are we?"

"This is the island," he said. "Remember? I told you to swim for it, then I swum but I didn't see you no more. I'm sorry I didn't try to help you, Cindy. Really I am."

She stared at her cousin, his wounds scabbed over, his one good eye peering through a milky film. His words and tone did not fit her memory of him. For a moment she entertained the notion she was still adrift and dreaming.

"I spent the night here—them little sandflies like to et me up, girl!—and this morning I was walking 'round the island when I saw you laying there. You musta washed up."

She nodded, then a hopeful thought struck her. "You haven't seen Grandpa, have you?"

He shook his head glumly. "He give his life for me, you know that?" His voice was low, suffused with shame.

She remembered the sight of her grandfather blindly throwing Calvin his life vest.

Calvin put his face in his hands and his body began to shake. "If only I could call it all back," he said, sobbing.

Instinctively she put her hand on his arm. "It's all right."

―――――――――

They watched the red sun set into the sea.

"Red sky at night, sailor's delight," Cindy said.

But with the sunset, nearly invisible sandflies began to bite them mercilessly.

"Come on," Calvin said. "They're not so bad on the other side."

She followed him down the beach, then along a path through sharp-edged bushes. On the other side of the island a stiff breeze whipped her clothes.

"Wind keeps them off," he said.

"Look." Cindy pointed to the lights of Pascagoula lining the coast a few miles away, across the Mississippi Sound.

"This is where I slept," Calvin said, making himself comfortable in the sand against a log. Cindy followed suit.

"We'll get off tomorrow," she said confidently. They had seen several boats before dark, but none close enough to signal.

"I hope so. I'm starving," he said.

"Haven't you been able to find any food?"

He laughed. "This island's pint-sized. Ain't a half-mile long, I guess. I walked all around it. Lighthouse down there hasn't been used in years. And that bit of jungle isn't nothing but pine trees, briars, and cactus."

"Where did you get the water?"

"There's a little swamp in there."

"If we don't get off tomorrow I'll find us some food," Cindy said, not sure where her confidence came from.

"I don't reckon it matters anyhow," Calvin said. "My goose is cooked."

She looked at him questioningly.

"Harvey Blue," he clarified.

"What are you talking about?" she asked.

"You don't know? You really don't know?" He chuckled softly. "He's the old white man I offed."

"You mean you killed him?"

He nodded.

A prickle went down her back. "Why did you kill him, Calvin?"

He shrugged, peering out across the dark sea to the moving headlights of cars along the coastal highway. "Uncle Nick was right. I had evil in me. That's all I know."

"And you don't now?"

He lay back, hands clasped behind his head, propped against the log for a view of the sea. "I don't know. Maybe that old man was right. I mean about his Bible and Jesus and all. Anyway, look where it all got me. I'm just real sorry about what I did to you. I can't expect you to believe it, though."

Cindy's skin felt raw, her body all out of kilter. She was still thirsty and dizzy, and hunger grew inside her. But she shook off her pains, remembering the lessons she had learned adrift.

"It doesn't matter what I believe," she said.

———

She slept under a blanket of wind, wakened frequently by sharp insect bites as sandflies managed to find spots on her flesh out of the wind where they could nibble her. Eventually the air became still and she detected light beyond her closed eyelids, but she did not want to open her eyes and face another day—not just yet.

She dozed intermittently in the light of the morning sun, licking her dry lips, turning over in her sleep and hearing Calvin shift and sigh a few feet away on the cool sandy beach.

A shadow fell across her. She opened her eyes.

Two uniformed men carrying rifles stood over her. One put a finger to his lips. The other took a pair of handcuffs from his belt and, leaning over Calvin, snapped them into place.

"Huh?" Calvin sat up, blinking and frowning.

"Would you look at that face," one of the men said.

Glancing at Calvin, Cindy realized she had become accustomed to his face.

"Come on, get up," the officer said. "You okay, ma'am?"

Cindy nodded, rising stiffly.

"Boat's on the other side. Let's go."

"Well, cousin," Calvin said. He almost smiled before the officer prodded him down the beach.

CHAPTER 28

The nurse tapped gently on the door, easing it open.

"Mr. Rose? You've got a visitor. Go on in," she whispered to Cindy.

Nick lay in bed, an IV attached to his arm, his eyes neatly bandaged.

"Grandpa?" Cindy said softly, walking to his side.

"Cindy? Cindy, is that you girl?" He sat up awkwardly as she leaned forward to hug him.

"Sweet Jesus," he said, sitting back. "I never thought I'd meet you on earth again, girl."

"I didn't either, Grandpa," she snuffled.

"Is there anybody else in here? Is that nurse in here?"

"No, Grandpa. It's just me," Cindy said.

He held both her hands in his. "How did you make it, honey? Tell me what happened."

She told him the story in brief. "But how did you make it, Grandpa? I mean without a life vest?"

"I'm a good swimmer. I swum across the Mississippi River one time on a bet. I just shucked my clothes and stayed a-floating, and by and by the Lord sent a boat by and I hollered 'em in. They picked me up and I made 'em hunt for you and Calvin, I sure did, but we didn't have no luck—till now."

"What did the doctors say—about your eyes, I mean?"

He shook his head and smiled. "I'm Blind Nick Rose now, like all them famous bluesmen you keep asking me about."

"Oh, Grandpa."

"Being blind don't bother me a bit, girl—not now that I can see. I mean really see. You know what I mean?"

She laughed and leaned over him, pulling him close. Tears ran down her face. "Yes, I know what you mean," she murmured into his ear. "I know."

━━━━━━━━

Bartram Oliver closed his notepad. "That's an amazing story, Cindy. I'm afraid this is going to beat our previous article all to pieces."

She smiled. She had felt more relaxed during this interview, no longer afraid of seeming the enthusing, effusing girl. Still, she couldn't keep the excitement out of her voice during parts of the story.

"In fact, I may see if I can get this in the *American*," Bartram added, referring to the Hattiesburg newspaper. "This is real news, Cindy."

"Hey, maybe it will help your career," she said.

"Yeah, and yours too. The next Connie Chung makes her media debut." They both chuckled, and he added, "I've got to meet this grandfather of yours. He sounds fantastic."

"He is. I'll take you out there one day. You'd love him. He's so—"

186

"Diverse?"

Cindy laughed. "I don't know if that quite describes Grandpa."

"Your cousin, though—I don't know," Bartram said, shaking his head. "You say he's converted and everything, but still—"

"—but still, you wouldn't want to leave him alone with the kids," she finished for him.

Bartram chuckled nervously, but she continued solemnly, "I know exactly what you mean."

"I guess you of all people should know," he said, "after all he put you through."

"Yes. But I do believe he has changed. Who can measure those things, though? Calvin's not a normal person, obviously. Maybe he has a chemical imbalance in the brain, or maybe it was the way he was brought up."

"Maybe he's just plain bad."

"Whatever. I sincerely believe he has changed for the better. I'm glad he's in jail, though. That's where he needs to be, for his own sake as well as everybody else's."

"Do you think he's still dangerous?"

"Only God knows that."

"Have you seen him since he went to jail?"

"Once. I plan to visit him more, though. Poor Calvin needs all the help he can get."

"I'm just glad you made it out okay, Cindy. I still can't believe all you've been through. Boy, I can't wait to write this story."

She laughed. "It's good to be home, it really is." She wanted to add that it was good to see him again, too, but she held her tongue. Her ordeal in the swamp had precluded many thoughts of Bartram at the time, but seeing him again was wonderfully refreshing, like noticing the first flowers of spring after a long winter.

"Look, Cindy, this may not be a good time for me to ask this, but some jazz musicians are playing in town Friday and Saturday night, and I was wondering—"

"I'd love to," she said.

———

Nick sat on his front porch sipping from a pint jar of iced tea. Cindy walked up the steps and hugged him.

"Hello, Grandpa," she said.

He smiled at her. "Evenin', girl."

Dark sunglasses covered his eyes, and he wore a clean shirt and brand-new overalls, dark blue and stiff. Changes had occurred in her grandfather's household.

Over the hum of the air conditioner window unit Cindy heard the hysterically excited voices of game show contestants from a television set in the living room.

"How's Aunt Flossie?" she said, pulling up a chair.

Nick took a sip of tea, the ice cubes tinkling against the glass. "Fine, I guess."

After much discussion among family members, it had been decided that one of Nick's daughters, Flossie, a widow, would move in with him to take care of him. But she only agreed to do it if certain changes were made—changes that most family members thought were long overdue anyway. Electricity. Plumbing. Appliances: television, air conditioning, washing machine, dryer.

Nick had shelled out a bundle, but it was either that or hire a nurse or even enter a nursing home, so he readily complied. He didn't mind much, anyway, and he enjoyed having ice.

"The book and the guitar are just inside the door," Nick told Cindy—as if she didn't know. "Get you some tea while you're in there."

"Hey, Aunt Flossie," Cindy said as she stuck her head in the door.

Flossie grunted from the flickering gloom, a dour woman in her fifties whose main interests lay in soap operas and game shows. Cigarette smoke curled through the room.

Cindy took the book and the guitar and went back out, closing the door softly so as not to interfere with the program.

"Now, where were we last time?" she said, leaning the guitar against a post and sitting down with the book.

"Second Samuel—the part about Absalom," Nick replied happily. As she opened the book, he asked, "How's Calvin?"

"Good," she said. "He really liked the large-print Bible. Said he's never been a good reader and that would help him."

Nick nodded. Calvin awaited trial in the county jail—guarded closely in a separate cell since his legendary escape. But Cindy believed he had no intention of fleeing.

"Did you tell him to read about Saint Paul, in Acts, how he was in jail too?" Nick asked.

"I forgot, Grandpa. I'll be sure and tell him next time."

In addition to visiting Calvin in jail, Cindy had made it a point to seek out Tom Hunt, the swamp hermit. She wanted to make certain he was all right after Calvin's attack and also to thank him.

With the help of maps and a full tank of gasoline, she finally located the dirt road that led to the landing where she had first met him. From there she set out on foot to find his shack, wearing high boots and carrying a compass for security.

She found the house with little trouble. It was empty, but did not look abandoned. She perched herself on the wooden steps above the water and waited. But despite her alert vigil, she jumped at the sound of his voice.

"Who's that?" he hollered across the swamp, poking his rifle barrel around the cypress trunk.

She grinned in relief, standing and waving her arms. "It's me," she said. "It's just me."

When he recognized her, he lowered his gun and approached with that awful, rotten-toothed grin of his. "I knew I'd see you again," he declared. "I learnt it in a dream."

They sat side by side on the steps as she told him her story and he told her his. He wanted to take her crawfishing but the day was growing late, so he contented himself by making her take a gunnysack full of live crawfish he'd already caught.

"Second Samuel," her grandfather prompted, bringing her back to the present.

Cindy began to read about the tragedy of King David who, having lost his son Absalom, grieved over him even though he had been wicked and treacherous.

She and her grandfather had a new ritual these days. Instead of bringing him whiskey in exchange for blues, she read to him from the Bible, after which he would play for her. She had started at Genesis and planned to read straight through to Revelation. She'd had a hard go of it with Leviticus, Numbers, and Deuteronomy, but ever since Judges it had been smooth sailing. Not that her grandfather minded any of it. He frequently found meaning in passages that to her seemed impenetrable.

"Mighty fine, mighty fine," he said when she had finished reading, shaking his glass of ice cubes thoughtfully. "I like the one—how does it go? 'Thou hast given me thy shield—'"

"Thou hast also given me the shield of thy salvation: and thy gentleness hath made me great," Cindy read. "That's Second Samuel 22:36. And I like this one, Grandpa, back in verse 34: 'He maketh my feet like hinds' feet: and setteth me upon my high places.'"

Nick nodded. "That's mighty purty too." He paused. "What's hinds' feet, Cindy girl?"

"Deer, I think, Grandpa. Just like the deer around here."

"Mighty fine, mighty fine," he repeated, tinkling his glass. "How's about you go get us some more tea while I tune up?"

"Sure, Grandpa." She went in, tiptoeing quickly

across the television's path into the kitchen, where she refilled his glass and poured one for herself.

Back outside, the rich, muted sound of the guitar filled the porch and spilled out into the thick summer air. Taking the jar, her grandfather paused for a drink, and Cindy sat back in her chair, holding her tea glass in both hands, gazing out into the green yard and, beyond it, the dark wall of pine forest.

Nick set his glass down, cleared his throat, and strummed a chord. E-seventh. The prettiest sound in the world. That B note, that D note, and that low rolling E.

Yessir.